According to Kovac

NewCon Press Novellas

Set 1: Science Fiction (Cover art by Chris Moore)
The Iron Tactician – Alastair Reynolds
At the Speed of Light – Simon Morden
The Enclave – Anne Charnock
The Memoirist – Neil Williamson

Set 2: Dark Thrillers (Cover art by Vincent Sammy)
Sherlock Holmes: Case of the Bedevilled Poet – Simon Clark
Cottingley – Alison Littlewood
The Body in the Woods – Sarah Lotz
The Wind – Jay Caselberg

Set 3: The Martian Quartet (Cover art by Jim Burns)
The Martian Job – Jaine Fenn
Sherlock Holmes: The Martian Simulacra – Eric Brown
Phosphorous: A Winterstrike Story – Liz Williams
The Greatest Story Ever Told – Una McCormack

Set 4: Strange Tales (Cover art by Ben Baldwin)
Ghost Frequencies – Gary Gibson
The Lake Boy – Adam Roberts
Matryoshka – Ricardo Pinto
The Land of Somewhere Safe – Hal Duncan

Set 5: The Alien Among Us (Cover art by Peter Hollinghurst)
Nomads – Dave Hutchinson
Morpho – Philip Palmer
The Man Who Would be Kling – Adam Roberts
Macsen Against the Jugger – Simon Morden

Set 6: Blood and Blade (Cover art by Duncan Kay)
The Bone Shaker – Edward Cox
A Hazardous Engagement – Gaie Sebold
Serpent Rose – Kari Sperring
Chivalry – Gavin Smith

Set 7: Robot Dreams (Cover art by Fangorn)
According To Kovac – Andrew Bannister
Deep Learning – Ren Warom
Paper Hearts – Justina Robson
The Beasts Of Lake Oph – Tom Toner

According to Kovac

Andrew Bannister

NewCon Press
England

First published in the UK by NewCon Press
41 Wheatsheaf Road, Alconbury Weston, Cambs, PE28 4LF
March 2020

NCP223 (limited edition hardback)
NCP224 (softback)

10 9 8 7 6 5 4 3 2 1

According to Kovac copyright © 2020 by Andrew Bannister

Cover art copyright © 2020 by Fangorn

All rights reserved, including the right to produce this book, or portions thereof, in any form.

ISBN:

978-1-912950-48-5 (hardback)
978-1-912950-49-2 (softback)

Cover art by Fangorn
Cover layout by Ian Whates

Minor Editorial meddling by Ian Whates
Final Text layout by Storm Constantine

One

Down here, they call me Kovac.

I come out of my fugue. I'm sitting where I was when I went into it, maybe five minutes ago, with my back pressed against a tree-trunk, staring upwards into a black bowl of sky with the stars of the Mandate spread across it. It's a hot, close night and there's no wind. I can smell my own sweat.

It takes me about an hour to walk up here from the city. The ground is dry, sucked to dust by the thirsty roots of the screw-pines. The trees aren't native; they were planted a century ago to stabilise the slope before the city was built below it.

The slope is stable, all right. It's also as dry as the end of time. The trees give off a sharp, sweetly chemical smell that almost drowns even my own rank scent. It's their sap. It burns like rocket fuel. Every couple of seasons the whole mountainside goes up in a firestorm that makes such a draft it pulls the roofs off the houses down below.

But since no one important lives in the houses, no one important cares enough to do anything.

It's a hard walk, and not just because of the slope which is never less than one in five. The dryness and the fires have cooked the soil down to a slick flour, just a few hand's breadths deep above the almost universal peat that forms the substrate of these floating islands. Your feet keep slipping, just a bit, so your muscles are always on the twitch to compensate. It makes them ache.

That's probably why I've always tended to assume I had the place to myself.

But it's worth the effort to see the stars. You can't see them clearly from down below. You have to get away from the sullen streetlights and well above the two big chimneys of the power plant, with the wobbling grey haze of sooty smoke that always hangs round them and spreads out to seal the city in its bowl, scooped out of the peat by the waves a thousand years ago, like a poisonous lid.

Unavoidable, say the important people. The business of this island is generating electricity. Not that they spend any of the profits on updating the power plant. But then they don't live down there on Craft Krasp. They live on another island, Grand Krasp, that follows this one around, five hundred metres upwind at the end of two massive tow chains.

There are several such inequitable pairings on this drowned planet, but everyone tells me this is the most unequal of all. I can believe them.

I need to see the stars. Not every night, and anyway I wouldn't have time for that. But a few times a month, at least, when the wheeling stars are in the right place — if only to remind myself that there is something outside this strange little planet.

Of course, that isn't my only reason. But it's the one I give if anyone asks.

It's getting late. I can hear a dry rattling noise — the flat-bugs, heading for their burrows around the exposed roots at the bottoms of the trunks. And if they're heading underground, it means other things are coming, and a few of those things will take a bite of you if they get the chance. It's time I was gone. Besides, I've done what I came here to do, and the trip back down is worse in the dark.

I stand up and push myself away from the trunk, at the same time turning my eyes down from the brightness of the stars. My sight adapts; I locate the ghostly grey thread of the path and begin to walk.

The trees thin out as I drop towards the pollution cloud and the rattling of the bugs fades. For a few hundred careful paces, until I am low enough for the night noises of the city to begin to intrude, the only sound is the soft scuff of my feet.

And, when I stop for a moment, a single quiet step that I didn't take, somewhere off to my right.

Well, well. Not so alone as I thought.

There's no point hanging around, so I start walking again. The warm still air has made the smoke layer more pungent than usual. I grab for the cloth hanging from my belt and press it to my face, thankful that it's still slightly damp. The locals don't seem troubled by the stuff but even after years here I'm not used to it.

After a few hundred eye-stinging metres I'm through the worst and I can take the cloth away from my face. I'm among the first houses now, and my feet know the way.

But I still falter, and then stop. I can hear distant shouted orders, and other shouts that are not orders but more like protests. Or pleas. And I can hear revving motors, and then a shot, somewhere a long way in front of me.

I start to run. As I get closer to the noise there are other people running, mostly towards me. Away from the shouts and the engines. I should be following them, but I'm not.

By the time I get to The Street of Steps the noise has stopped and I slow to a walk. The street is empty, apart from Pas, who is sitting in his usual broken chair outside our door, smoking his pipe.

He's doing his best to look relaxed, but I can tell from the scent of the smoke that the pipe has only just been lit, and from where the legs have left fresh scrape-marks in the sooty dust on the street. He's turning something over in his hand – a little leaf of silver metal like an ornament, but as I approach he puts it in his pocket.

I squat down beside him. 'Another sweep?'

He nods, making the pipe wag. 'Big one. I saw ten wagons. Must have cost a fortune in oil. Ironic, considering it was ostensibly prompted by an oil riot.'

I draw a breath. Each wagon takes ten people seated – forty standing. Pas was right. This had been big.

I flick my eyes upwards in question towards the house behind him. He shakes his head, and some of the tension drains from me. Not us then. Not this time.

Pas gives me his twisted smile. 'What about you? Staring at the stars again?'

'Yes.'

'Anyone disturb you?'

'No. I'd know.' And I would. My fugue state is deep but watchful, liked a waking dream; anyone coming close to me might as well be hauling on a trip-wire.

He nods. 'Nor follow you?'

I hesitate, and he grins. He's not without his own senses. 'I'm not sure.'

'If you're not sure, that means you were.'

'Perhaps.' I tell him about the footfall.

When I have finished he is quiet for a moment. Then he shrugs. 'That sounds amateurish, and I don't believe it. If you want my guess, I'd say that someone wants you to *think* you were followed this time, and that since this is the first time you noticed, it's the first time you've been followed. And that means, my boy, that it almost certainly isn't.'

'Why would they do that?'

'Do what? Follow you, or play with your head?'

'Either.'

'How can I tell? Any idea who it might be?'

'No.'

The lie comes too easily, but this time Pas doesn't seem to notice. He counts on his fingers. 'One, you've crossed a line in love and someone wants your hide. No?'

'No.'

'Two, you owe someone a lot of money. No?'

I laugh, actually meaning it. 'In my state that would be something of an ambition.'

'I thought so. It only leaves politics.'

I shake my head. 'I don't do politics, Pas.'

'Neither did most of a hundred and fifty people, I daresay. Complaining about the price of oil should hardly count. But there they went just now, off in the wagons.'

I don't need to ask how he found out the number so quickly. Word moves along these narrow streets faster than wagons. Faster than anything except fear.

But a hundred and fifty? I shake my head. 'Why so many?'

'Who knows? And something else, Kovac. They were mostly young.'

He lets the word fall towards the street like a drop of poison.
I stare at him for a moment. Then I say, carefully, 'That's new.'
'Yes.'
'But they still didn't come to us.'
'No. Our little waifs are safe tonight.'
'Why?'
He looks up, his eyes flashing. 'You think I know the answer? Ask them.'
'They don't exist.'
He says nothing, but twists his lip at the joke.

Even the most benign state sometimes needs some unofficial help; someone to do the awkward things that need to be done. The bad things.

The Mutual Island State of Grand and Craft Krasp is not benign. Officially they have a police force, a special police force, and an intelligence service, all above board and all supposedly devoted to the safety of the people who must therefore be the safest people in the Mandate.

But their other help is called the Jeremiad. And officially, it doesn't exist. Ministers and Counsellors will deny it flat, in public and on record. The big, ugly, anonymous building with the small windows on the Street of Fleshmen, the one people cross the road to avoid, doesn't contain them, and if anyone is ever questioned to death, it can't have been them because they don't exist.

People say they have an even bigger place on Grand Krasp, but the only people who can know if that is true are never going to be able to tell.

They held Pas for six months, years ago, before I met him. He always says that's when he learned how to be old, but he never says anything else.

Jeremiad means Lamentation. It's a good name

Pas has a far-away look now, so I leave him to his memories and walk into the house. It's an old town house, strongly built the way they used to here when anyone could still afford to. A couple of centuries old, it's a squat dirty-grey tower of pre-cast concrete cuboids stacked on top of each other, slightly offset so they create overhangs and balconies at each storey. There used to be metal railings on the balconies, but Pas sold them ten years ago when he ran out of money for a while. Now there are wobbly timber fences with every plank a different colour and shape and having different parentage. It looks cheerful, in a ragged kind of a way.

Pas used to talk about buying back the railings, late evenings when he had had a few. Now he doesn't talk about anything much.

'Kovac! Finished star-staring?'

It's Fensh. My feet have taken me to the roof garden. She looks up from a salad bed and wipes a hand over her face, smearing a bit more soil over the older smears.

'You missed the sweep,' she says.

'You make it sound as if I missed a party. How are you, Fensh?'

'I'm fine, just as I was three hours ago. Before you went on your walk. Pas isn't.'

'I know. But he's pretending well.'

She smiles, but her eyes are serious. 'He thinks they will come for us too.'

'So far they haven't. They might not.' I don't like touching people, but she is radiating anxiety. I take her hands and draw her upright. Her head reaches my shoulder. 'You grow food for the kids, you tell them stories, you soothe Pas. You can't worry for us all as well, you know?'

The corners of her mouth turn down. 'You'll do that, will you?'

'I might as well do something. You make me feel lazy.'

'I know what you do.' She turns back to her work. Over her shoulder she says, 'Go and say hello to the others.'

I nod to her shoulders and go back inside.

At the moment there are eleven of them. More than usual, thanks to the Government. The number of adults here is shrinking slowly. Economic migration, partly, but that's slow and long term, and it's currently drowned out by the acute problem of parents disappearing in the night.

Either way, sooner or later the ratio of child to parent goes through a threshold and the kids spill onto the streets and stay there.

I suppose that's probably why Pas is tolerated. If he wasn't, the government would either have to look after them, or clean up the bodies.

I help when I can, as long as it doesn't mean doing anything that draws attention to me. That wouldn't help at all.

I used not to dream, before, because my kind don't, but they warned me that now I might. The container shapes the contents, they said.
It seemed a risk worth taking. And so I dream.
In my dream I'm looking at the starfield, half-familiar from my evening walk, but this time it is all around me so that I am utterly immersed in it. I am connected to a thousand eyes and ears and other senses as well. I can taste the lonely gas molecules that float around me; I can feel the singing spectra of the stars.
I am as I was – and it is about to happen again...
But instead I wake, because Fensh is shaking my shoulder. She steps back as my eyes open.
'Sorry...'
I sit up and wave a hand. 'It's fine.' And it is. She has saved me... 'What's the matter?'
'Someone's come. I think she's ill. Please?'
I follow her. The house is a maze of small rooms and many corridors. I once saw a castle made that way; built for defensibility. I keep meaning to ask Pas about it, but every time something distracts me. This time it is a young woman, or perhaps a girl, it's hard to tell. She is lying on a cot in one of those small rooms, and the first thing I notice is her breathing. It is the gasp – hold – sigh – pattern of someone who is making a supreme effort, over and over again.
The second thing is her belly. She is very pregnant. I lay a hand on her forehead, and pause.
Right. I turn to Fensh. 'Go and make hot water, and bring clean cloths.'
Her eyes widen, but she gives a professional nod. 'The stove is still hot,' she says. And she leaves the room.
When I am sure she is gone I turn to the girl – because that is the right term. I would guess about fourteen standard years. My hand is still on her forehead, and it is burning. 'You're safe,' I say. 'Talk to me.'
Another gasp, and the one word. 'Hurts.'
I press harder on the clammy skin. 'I know. Where? How long?'

'Here, and here. Two days.' Her hand has sketched circles over her belly, but also her hips.

My chest tightens. 'You have been pushing for two days?'

She nods.

'And the pain? The same for two days?'

Another nod.

'Very well. How long?'

'Eight months.' She lets the words out on another gasp.'

Premature, then, but not by much. 'What's your name?'

Her lips compress. No name, then. I smile, hoping she can see it in the dim light, and say, 'We will take care of you. You will be fine.'

She shuts her eyes, but the skin around them seems a little more relaxed. Good; I will indeed look after her as best I can, and I truly hope she will be fine.

As for the child, I do not need to investigate further to know that it is already dead. And if something is not done soon, so will be the mother.

I keep my hand on her forehead until Fensh comes in with water and cloths. Some things I know how to do because I set out to learn then when I first came here – seeking what in return, I am still not sure – and with Fensh's help I do them until the girl with no name is free of her burden and sleeping.

Fensh watches her for a moment. 'Will she be okay?'

'I believe so. Her fever is already a little lower. And she is young. She will heal well.'

'Good. Thank you, Kovac.'

'I wish I could have done more.' We have covered the dead foetus with some of the cloths. I gesture towards it. 'But that – there was never any hope for that.'

'Yes. I don't want to look at it again.'

I reach out and rub her shoulder. She feels tense. 'Then don't. There's no need.'

'Yes. Kovac? I've never seen anything like that before.'

'Nor have I.' And I hope I never do again, I add to myself. Out loud I say, 'You should go and sleep. She will need someone like you when she wakes. Not someone like me. Go on. Rest.'

She hesitates. 'Will you stay with her?'

'Of course.'

I wait until the door has closed behind her before I take hold of the cloth and uncover the foetus. That is the right word. The thing is not – was never – a baby or a child. It is roughly human-shaped, but too many things are wrong. The wrong limbs in the wrong places. Barely developed eyes, despite being apparently eight months. Something that looks like an external heart.

Colossal genetic abnormality. No wonder the girl was ill. I wonder how she managed to carry the pregnancy for so long – but I wonder even more what caused it.

These people are robust. Birth abnormalities are rare, which is why Fensh has never seen one. Partly that's because of the environment – they haven't invented complex chemicals or anything radioactive yet, and at the rate they're going they never will.

But nothing like that can have been causeless.

There's no way of testing for what it was without leaving the planet, and that is not an option. I take a long look to fix the poor thing in my mind, pull the cloth back over it, and pick up the bundle. It must be gone before the girl wakes; anything else would be cruelty. So I pad quietly down the corridors to the basement furnace. Pas is asleep down there, mumbling on his cot. He doesn't rouse when I hitch open the furnace door, slip the bundle into the dull, red, peat-smelling interior, and latch the door behind it.

There; gone.

I go back to the girl's room. She, too, doesn't wake. I sit down in the chair next to her pallet and close my eyes. Not for sleep, because I know that isn't going to happen.

For thinking.

This planet is called Kasapt and, without knowing as much, it is an experiment. It is the best observed planet in the Mandate, and despite that, or perhaps because of it, nobody here has ever heard of the Mandate.

Ten thousand years ago Kasapt was a middle-sized planet with a surface covered about eighty percent by water, with two big polar ice caps and two big low-lying land masses topped mainly by peat, except where they were covered by moss that was on its way to being peat.

It had a hydrocarbon economy based on the peat, and on the oil and bitumen deposits underneath it, and it was happily unaware of the rest of the universe; a pragmatic people knew that the lights in the sky were stars and planets, but they had all the oil and peat they needed right here, so why go anywhere else?

The rest of the Universe, or anyway the emerging Mandate, had grown out of oil and peat and had other things on its mind, so the pragmatic people of Kasapt were left in peace to burn their own geology in their own good time.

It took them five hundred years of industrialisation to burn their way to the point where both ice caps melted, and they were the large ice caps of a cool temperate planet. Ninety-five percent of the land was submerged. The rising water tore great shelves of peat from the inundated land. Just light enough to float, it formed the ragged floating islands that are most of the land now.

The population fell from just over a billion to less than three million in the space of a single millennium.

This was when the Mandate took an interest. Not an active interest, because it was too late for that, but a watchful interest. Even scholarly. What was going to happen next, and could it be predicted?

So Kasapt's existing isolation was made formal. Do not touch, do not contact. Rival universities, government agencies and a few who were too shy to disclose themselves spent a lot of money buying orbital slots and filling them with smart remote sensing, and the data poured out and was argued over.

All very fine. But if you really want to understand the feel, the smell and the taste of a society you have to be in it, undetected, at ground level.

That's where I come in. And others, too. I know I'm not alone, but that's all I know. Who, where and how many, I have no idea. And they don't know about me either.

I hope.

I was right that sleep didn't happen, but a sort of exhausted stupefaction did, so I didn't notice the daylight, or Fensh coming in to the room carrying a tray. She is just – there, smiling at me.

'All quiet?'

'Yes. Did you sleep?'

Her face clouds. 'A little. Not very well. Every time I closed my eyes I saw – it.' She glances at the table. 'Is it...?'

She means the foetus. I nod.

'Good.' And she puts the tray down where the bundle had been. 'Take a cup if you want one, but then you should go. She's stirring.'

I looked at the girl, and saw her frown and change position. 'Yes,' I say. 'I'll go.'

I don't wait for a drink.

It's a sunny morning, which means that the smog layer is glowing a creamy colour and the air below is warm and stagnant. I still need the drink, and I need to walk, and I need news. I know I won't get it by asking, but I might get it by listening.

I walk for twenty minutes, heading generally towards the centre of the town. The crowds thicken. I choose a stall halfway down a street lined with them; take a stool under the canopy and accept a cup of the only thing they sell, an infusion made from the flowers of the ubiquitous moss. The drink is so common they don't even name it. It is just 'a drink'.

And I watch and listen, and I begin to get the flavour of the crowd. Normal, but not normal. Everyone is not saying all the things they're not allowed to say, but they're not saying them pretty loudly.

The raid shook them up. Not because raids are unusual – they're not. Half the population have been picked up, roughed up and let go again at some point in their lives. But this one was different. No one can remember anything that big, and no one can remember them going after children. Almost all of them female, it seems. I hadn't known that.

And we have a young female, turning up on the same night, in what the locals call a curious state. This troubles me.

Otherwise the grumbles of the people are as usual – mainly, now, the cost of lamp oil which has jumped again. It goes to explain the extra smoke, in part; in houses, people are going back to tallow and peat, and the power station is burning anything that can be reaped from the streets. It also goes to explain the protests. Oil is warmth and light and cooked food, just about all some of these people can hope for.

As I watch the crowd I become aware of someone watching me. I turn, and find myself looking into the eyes of the stallholder. He holds my gaze for a moment, then looks out over the people passing his stall. 'Busy this morning.'

'Yes.'

He pulls a cloth out of his belt and fusses it over the counter, which already looks averagely clean to me. 'Guessing some people didn't sleep well.'

'Perhaps so.'

'Yeah.' More fussing. 'You're the feller from the Street of Steps.'

It isn't a question, and I don't give an answer. I gaze over the crowd, but that's not where my attention is.

He takes my cup, which isn't empty yet, and re-fills it without being asked. 'Guess you must be wondering what's going on.'

Oh, I am, but I'm also wondering if I should just get up and walk off before I learn anything I don't want to know.

Instead I keep quiet.

The cup is hot, but I pick it up because I need to do something, to create movement. The metal counter underneath it bears a disc of moisture from the bottom of the cup and the stallholder reaches down, straightens a finger and makes a shape in the film. 'Take care of yourself,' he says, and then wipes the shape away.

But not before I've seen it. It was a 'J'.

It takes me a while to finish my drink, but the stallholder doesn't say another word. But the implied word Jeremiad is more than enough.

I get back to the house much faster than I left it. There's no sign of Pas, but Fensh hears me come in and comes to find me. Her face starts out welcoming and then changes when she sees mine. 'What's the matter?'

I pause, and rein myself in. Now is not the time to panic people – and Fensh would certainly catch my panic, very easily. She doesn't need to know that the Jeremiad have been rounding up girls.

I rein myself in all over again. *Might* have been. *Rumoured* to have been. I'm panicking myself. So I make myself smile. 'Sorry, Fensh. I'm tired. How's our guest?'

'As good as you'd think. She seems fair enough, but she's upset.'

'Yes. Well, she would be.' I pause. 'Does she have a name yet?'

She gives a sideways grin. 'She hasn't said. But while she slept I took her clothes to wash. There's a House Mark in them. A Great House.'

My heart speeds up. 'Do you recognise it?'

'No. It's not from one of the near Islands, that's all I know.'

'I see. Well, can I talk to her?'

'If she's awake. I gave her a big draught of the dark syrup. Come on.'

I follow her, my heart still racing. I am hoping for the best, whatever that might be. Possibly that the girl has stolen those clothes, or bought them from a thief, or found them. Anything, as long as it means we don't really have a recently pregnant refugee from a distant Great House on our hands just when the Jeremiad is unexpectedly interested in girls.

Might be, I try to tell myself, but I have run out of conviction.

Our guest is sitting up on her cot with clean linen under her – Fensh must have found time to change that – and she's wearing one of Fensh's smocks. In the daylight her face is pale, and there are bruise shadows on one cheek.

The life of a House girl. One with watchful eyes.

Fensh leans against the wall by the door. I gesture at the cot. 'May I?'

The girl nods, and I sit down. She looks less drugged that I expected – dark syrup is an powerful and illegal blend of opiates. Fensh grows the seeds on the roof and mills them in the kitchen, and I can never understand how she gets away with it.

'How are you,' I ask.

'Well, thank you. Are you Kovac?'

'Yes.'

'She says you made me better.'

She is Fensh. 'Yes. Well, we both did. Do you hurt anywhere?'

'I'm sore and my head feels light. What did you do with my...' The words dry up, but she holds my eyes a little angrily.

'I'm sorry. Your child was dead – had died inside you. It could never have lived. I don't know how you carried it as long as you did.

Any longer, and you would have died with it.'

The eyes flinch. 'Have you done away with it?'

I nod.

'Well then. I can leave.' She pauses. 'What was it like?'

I take a moment to think. I have never had a child. I don't know what I would be thinking and feeling – but these people are tough, and House girls especially. I decide on plainness. 'It was poorly formed, as if made from the wrong things. It did not look like a child. I am sorry.'

She is sharp. 'It wasn't your child. And you don't know me. Why should you be sorry?'

Strong, and also proud. I say nothing. From the doorway Fensh says, 'Is there anyone you will need to tell?'

The girl laughs. 'I was going to, but now I won't. I wouldn't give him the satisfaction.'

I turn to look at Fensh. She is smiling a little. 'Does that mean he doesn't know yet,' she says.

'That's right. He always gave me a little thing to swallow before he had me. This time I kept it in my mouth.' She points a finger at her cheek. 'He never tried to kiss me. How could he know?'

Suddenly my mind is racing. These people practice birth control – pessaries, elaborate insertable devices, dangerous chemical potions and mass sterilisation – but as far as I know they have no workable oral contraceptive, and certainly nothing that would be given by the male to the female. Not getting pregnant is always *her* responsibility, not *his*.

So what was this little thing? And who was *he*?

I am still musing on that when the girl speaks again. 'The child,' she says. 'Did it seem... human?'

And my racing mind slams to a stop, and in the trembling quiet that follows I hear my own voice say, quite calmly, 'What do you mean, human?'

'We used to wonder about him. If he would get human children. That's why I kept the thing in my mouth. To find out. And I thought...' Then her eyes glaze for a second. She flinches, and presses a hand to her belly.

Fensh is at her side. 'Is it hurting more?'

The girl nods. 'And my head… dizzy.'

'Here.' Fensh reaches into her smock and pulls out a little phial. 'Five drops… There. You'll be better soon.'

I raise my eyebrows. She certainly will. The dose is enough to drop a peat-cutter in his tracks.

The girl catches the tiny drops on a pale tongue, then sinks back and smiles. I lean forward. 'What were you saying about human children?'

'Wanted to find out.' The words are already slurred.

'Find out what?'

Her eyes have closed. She opens them a little and looks at me. 'See if the child would be a God.'

She gives a contended little sigh and slumps a little to the side. Fench lays a hand on her forehead and then her belly. 'No fever or bloat,' she says, 'but I'm not sure she's right. I'm worried that she's dizzy. What do you think she meant?'

'I have no idea. Perhaps it was the syrup talking.'

'Perhaps.' Fensh's face is neutral. 'Perhaps it will talk some more later.'

She pulls covers over the sleeping girl and smooths them down, while I watch her.

I suddenly want to know, very much indeed, where this girl has come from.

The sun is dead overhead when I leave the house for the second time in one day. The smoke layer is beginning to invert, so later on we should have a good photochemical smog to keep out the glare. For the moment, though, it's hot and unforgiving.

Earlier, I had been looking for gossip and atmosphere – for the eye that slides away, and the one that does not, and the flicker of someone's expression before they cross the street to avoid the question they are afraid you might ask. This time I have something specific in mind; the intricate little swirl of dots and lines of indelible green ink stamped into the lining of our sleeping guest's clothes.

The House Mark.

'Will you draw it?' Fensh had been reaching for a stub of pencil as she spoke.

'No. I'll remember it.'

'Really? I couldn't.' She gives me a curious look.

'I'm just lucky that way.' I pat her on the shoulder and leave before she can say anything else.

I certainly don't want to walk around with a picture of it in my pocket, not today, and besides, I don't need to. I know I'll remember it, and luck isn't involved.

Now I just need to find someone who can tell me what it means, which should be fairly easy – but without telling anyone else, which is not.

House Marks were probably easy and logical when they were first introduced. Each Great House ruled an Island, and each inhabited Island had one vote in the Great Assembly. Even to begin with there were anomalies, like Islands which had just a single inhabitant who spent only enough time there to maintain the fiction. But on a drowned planet where most of the islands were floating ones, and where floating today did not necessarily mean floating next week, the 'one float, one vote' connection was quickly broken. A vote was a valuable thing which could be bought or sold – or taken by force.

After hundreds of years of piracy, culminating in an outright war, the present arrangement was reached. Seventy-three Islands retained their votes, plus a further twenty-one votes which no longer represented any Island at all because they had sunk, or been sunk – and there were ten islands with no vote. The poor ones.

Kasapt has a vote, but it is exercised by the few hundred people who live on Grand Kasapt. As for us, we don't get a say.

Every time a vote changes hands, a Great House either gains or loses influence. Marks are combined, or split off as new Houses are founded by marriage or economic force. There are over a hundred Marks, and I have only learned a few of them because it has never mattered to me, until now.

So I carry the image of the little glyph in my head up the Street of Steps and along a zig-zag route around the bowl-shaped cityscape, dropping seawards as I go. As I get closer to the water the concrete buildings are replaced by a few made of stone, but many more of hard-compacted mud reinforced, after a fashion, with seaweed fibres. I start to smell the water, or it would be better to say, I start to smell what is in the water – sewage and dead things and dying things and oily tarry wastes from the power plant and the engine house, all trapped in the toxic soup of the bay by the inexorable tow-current.

I arrive at the waterfront, turn left and walk along the shore, breathing through my mouth and trying not to retch. Incredibly there are food stalls, and between them children play on short pipes for a few coins. I watch them filling their lungs to play the long phrases and think to myself, *how?*

And behind the children, something I am seeing more often – the lethargic forms of the Burst-smokers, staring or smiling or sleeping depending on when they last breathed in the hot fumes from the little twists of foil that sell for a day's food a time.

Then I turn away from the stinking water and the stinking children and the sleeping druggies because I have reached Further Chain Street.

The two great chains that bind us to Grand Kasapt curve up from the harbour at either side of the bay, nearly a kilometre apart. At the halfway point between the two islands they sometimes dip into the sea, but nearer the shore they are usually high enough for a ship to pass beneath if its mast is dipped. Exactly how far above ground they are depends on the weather and the towing speed – today they are easily thirty metres off the ground as they cross the edge of the docks, and they follow the streets up in long, condensation-soaked catenaries that fall form links bent from crude steel bar as thick as barrels, and spatter lines of rust on to cobbles now quite brown. Wrapped into the chains like strangling weeds are the power cables that export the output of our filthy generators to our wealthy neighbours.

The Further Chain follows the street, and I follow the chain until even the meanest houses have fallen away and I am walking up a narrowing chasm of concrete which ends where the chain plunges into a dark slot. Just outside the slot the cables unwind from the chains and swing up towards the power plant on mushroom-shaped glazed clay towers.

There is room for me beneath the chain, just.

A dozen paces inside, I stop and shut my eyes, silently counting to ten to allow my night vision to develop. As I pass 'seven' something brushes my face, and I smile. The bats form a first line of both detection and warning. Well then. I have been warned, and very shortly I will be announced.

Eyes open again, I walk forward cautiously. I think I know all the traps — but only think; it has been months since I was last here, and they have been uneasy months at that. The rising cost of oil, and therefore life; the growth of Burst as a social ill. Who sets less traps when times are uneasy?

And besides, I have no reason to assume that the person I may be walking towards is who I think they are. Things change.

Then, somewhere in front of me, someone uncovers a candle. I stop and wait.

'Who's that? Turn back! Let me die in peace.'

It is an old voice, thick with phlegm. It ends with a long, rich cough.

I spread my hands. 'You can see who I am.'

'The disease has taken my sight... Disease, I tell you! The Mud-Fever. My eyes, my lungs, soon my life. And yours, if you don't turn back.'

I smile. 'Mud-Fever, old woman? I'm impressed. Last time I visited you the worst thing I risked was wharf fleas.'

There is a pause. Then, 'Kovac?'

'Obviously.'

'There's nothing obvious about it. Don't move.' The candle flame wobbles towards me, and then I am facing an upright figure fully two heads shorter than me, and the light is glinting off two eyes shrouded in wrinkles.

I am studied for a while. Then the eyes are lowered and the candle flame makes a little circle. 'Apologies. I would wish to have trusted you sooner, but these days trust is even more fatal than old age, and it offers a much nastier death. Are you alone?'

'Of course.'

'There's no of course, same as there's no trust. Especially with some of the company you keep. Well, come on then. Follow me.'

The old figure turns, becoming a silhouette with an aura of candle-light. I follow, watching my step on the uneven floor and stooping a little to avoid knocking myself out on the chain, and wondering what company I keep that would worry anyone.

Ten paces further and we push through a heavy curtain that hangs down to the floor either side of the chain. The rust and damp smell changes to a sweet undertone of machine oil. Five paces more, and another curtain, and then I sense, rather than seeing, the space round me expand. The old voice says, 'You'd better close your eyes,' but I already have because I have been here before.

There is a brief electrical hum.

'You can open them now.'

I do so, slowly, keeping my gaze fixed on the floor until I have adjusted to the fierce industrial glare from a row of pendant globes hanging either side of the chain. Then I raise my eyes far enough to look into the quizzical face of the old woman in front of me. I am studied intently for a long moment. Then the old face relaxes.

'Hello, Kovac. It *is* you.'

'Yes. Hello, Sariast the Scholar.'

She raises her eyebrows. 'Full names, is it? Not fair, considering you've never confessed to yours.'

'You know all the names I have.'

'I doubt it. And you know more than I have, these days. I am scholar no more. Soon enough, nothing no more. Come and sit down. Don't bang your head.'

It's good advice. Above my head the chain soars across the big room and wraps round a huge reel, easily twenty metres across, with a fat spiral spring wound into its centre to adjust tension and absorb towing shocks. The spring always makes me think of something crouching, ready to leap. The whole thing moves, constantly, slightly and uneasily, winding a little in and out like breathing. A deep, almost subliminal groaning of bearings fills the chamber. The floor is strewn with cables and pieces of broken machine.

Sariast points to a couch in the far corner. 'Sit down. Then ask whatever it was you came to ask.'

I sit. 'How do you know I have a question?'

'Prove me wrong. Have you brought a present?'

'No...'

'And I'm too old for love and you're not interested in it anyway. Therefore, it's a question. Ask it.'

I laugh. 'Very well. I want to know about a House Mark.'

'Oh?' She looks at me sharply. 'Which one?'

'That's what I want to know.'

'I see. Show me.'

I shake my head. 'I don't have a copy. I can describe it.'

'Really?'

'Yes. Like this: All contained within a broken circle, two straight strokes horizon, above a three-quarter spiral right hand, tail down, three dots surmounting and the sign of waves around.'

She raises her eyebrows. 'Fluent heraldry, Kovac? Why do you need to ask me anything?'

'Because I can only describe it, not decipher it. Do you need to hear it again?'

'No. You captured it perfectly.' She stares at the ground for a moment, then looks up at me and smiles. 'House Marks are stories, you know? The waves around mean one of the fixed islands. A non-floater. Three dots surmounting signifies the division of the House – probably someone died and paid off some death duties with land. That they are surmounting rather than below means that the House is in the northern hemisphere. The two horizontal strokes are the remains of an older glyph of the original name of the island, and the tail-down spiral is a drill. And what do we drill for on an island?'

I answer the rhetorical question. 'Oil.'

'Good boy.' She falls silent.

I wait for a while, then lean forward. 'You've told me what and where, but not which.'

'Forgive me. I was thinking. It's the last pleasure of the very old.'

'Thinking about what?'

She looks up, and her old eyes pierce me. 'You really care nothing about love?'

I shake my head, confused. 'Perhaps. I don't know... Why?'

'You are an odd one, with your silence and your questions and your star-staring. I never met a man like you... Well, your Mark is of the Island Ganaft. Way up north. Isolationist. Doesn't bother voting, but buys votes anyway. Wealthy in oil, and getting wealthier as the supply gets short and the prices rise; I'd give you silver to bones that the lights above us are fuelled by Ganaft oil.'

I nod. 'Thank you.'

'You're welcome. Now answer me a question, if you will.'

'If I can.'

'I am sure you can... Why would you be asking me about Ganaft House Marks only three days after a Ganaft barge docked?'

There's no trust. I think fast. 'Barges must dock all the time, if we use that much oil.'

'They do. But they discharge *only* oil – and less than they used to. Not people – until three days ago.'

I nod slowly. 'And then one did?'

'So I am told – and you didn't answer.' Her eyes have been fixed on mine, immobile, but now she blinks and the tension drops. 'I don't go out any more, you know? But people come to me. Sometimes they talk.'

I smile. 'And sometimes they bring presents?'

'I live in hope.' She laughs, and I hear the rough, wet edge to the sound. 'But sometimes they bring news. It keeps me going. Has kept me going.'

'Long may it last,' I say without conviction, because her skin is pale and slack, and the wet rasp of her laugh is still there as an uneasy background to her breathing. I lean closer. 'Should I bring someone?'

'Only if they like lost causes. Kovac? The world is changing. It wasn't good to begin with but it is changing for the worst. The oil, the drugs. I won't always be tolerated down here. I'm old enough not to care, but one day it may be that they come for me. I won't go quietly, when they do. And I'll leave 'em something to remember me by.'

I watch her for a while, and she submits to the scrutiny with something like resignation. I wonder how old she is, and where she came from, and if anyone will be troubled when she dies, but those are questions I can't ask. Instead I say, 'Is the barge still here?'

'The last I heard, yes. Look for *Silent Sentinel.* But don't look out loud, and don't tell anyone.'

'I won't. Are you sure I can't do anything?'

'Of course, fool. And Kovac? I mean it. Be careful who you talk to, and have a good journey.'

'What journey?'

'Suit yourself. I'm tired.' And she turns away.

There's nothing else to say, so I stand and, after a pause, walk out of the chamber and back along the narrow passage with the chain above my head. I'm expecting a bat to follow me, but instead there is silence in the passage.

But not in my head. Because I had never told the old woman about staring at the stars. And nor had she told me about the cloth-wrapped tubes, each the thickness of an arm, that are wrapped round two links of the Chain. They hadn't been there last time.

Something to remember, indeed.

Outside, the afternoon is drawing to a close. The quay won't get hotter or smellier than this. Even the peat-tar on the old planks underfoot is sticky with heat, and the children have put away their pipes and their begging bowls and are snoozing in any patches of shade they can find. Only those in a Gift coma are still in the sun, their skin baking to blotched scarlet.

The Manifold Dock is halfway along the curve of the harbour where the water is deepest. A floating pontoon, thirty paces across, that extends five hundred paces out from the shore, it is supported by metal buoys and rafts of spongewood and the still-floating hulls of abandoned hulks and anything that was above water when it was built, and the centre of it is weighed down by two pipes of tarred canvas that collapse to slack sheets when they are empty, but swell to obscenely pulsating members when someone is pumping oil.

Someone is pumping now. The canvas slug nearest me is swollen and writhing, and even in the hot weather I can feel the heat pouring off it – the thick crude oil needs to be hot if it is to flow, and even then it flows slowly. I follow the pontoon out almost to the end and the last vessel, riding high in the water to expose a three-metre band of weed, is the *Silent Sentinel.*

It is enormous, easily the biggest vessel I have ever seen on this planet. I guess it at well over two hundred metres long and fifty wide, and on the slime-coated band of hull that has reared up out of the water as the oil is pumped away I see lines of bulges.

Rivets. This behemoth is made of steel – and that means it is old; ancient, even, because as far as I know this planet has not been able to roll steel plates on this scale for a thousand years.

Not bad, for an isolationist island up north.

'Not bad, eh?'

The voice is behind me. I turn and see a skinny man wearing a docker's cap. His eyebrows are raised, as if he is waiting for an answer.

'Yes. Not bad. Where does she come from?'

He spreads his arms. 'Who knows? When she goes, she heads across the tow blast and then her smoke goes due east.'

'You've seen her before then?'

'Ay-uh. She's back every two-month with another belly-full of the black stuff. Used to be every month, but there's less and less of it these days. And she rides higher when she turns up. Not so full, see?' He grins. 'I watch the ships, I do.'

I nod. 'And the people?'

'Ah. On a time, if there are people to watch. And people to tell, mebbe?'

He licks his lips. The moisture emphasises their dryness, and now that I look properly I can see that the skin round his eyes is slack and sunken, and his faded cap has a darker patch, puncture-edged where a badge has been torn away.

Light dawns. An *ex*-docker, then. Guildless, and therefore workless, and perhaps hungry. Or thirsty.

I wave a hand upwards towards the glaring sun. 'It's hot. Where's a good place to drink?'

His eyes light up, and he gestures me along the pontoon.

We are in the back bar of the Ploughed Furrow, which I have heard of but always avoided until today, and the ex-docker has acquired a name – Vekam – and a slim bottle of the dirty brown spirit they brew here from grain leftovers. The bottle is now only half full, but the meat pie on the plate in from of him is pristine. I suspect he has made the safer choice.

I watch him take another swallow, and then lean forwards. 'The *Silent Sentinel*, then.'

'The what?' He wipes his lips.

'The big boat that sails east. Do you see people come from her?'

'Ah. No. they keep their own company.'

'Really?' I'm tempted to snatch the bottle from him, but I've already paid for it and I certainly have no use for it myself. 'What do they do then?'

He leers. 'How should I know? Anything they can do on board. Each other, shouldn't wonder. Sailors, see.'

Now I do reach out, and my hand closes around the bottle before he can pull it away. 'I didn't come here for dirty stories,' I say.

'I ain't told any, yet.' He glares at me for a moment, then subsides. 'What I told you. They keeps their own company, whoever they are. Stay on board. I hardly even sees 'em. Never a coin for a bit of help. Even when the bumboat comes, they just haul the provisions up in nets. Reckon I only ever see a couple of men on deck.'

I let go of the bottle and he pulls it close to him. 'Men, eh,' I say. 'Never women?'

His eyes widen. 'You lost your mind? Grown bints on a boat? Recipe for war.'

'I suppose so.' I watch him for a moment, then stand up. 'You've been helpful.'

'Not yet, I ain't. You want value out of your booze, you should ask the right questions.'

I remain standing. 'Such as?'

'You asked about women. You dint ask about lads.'

I sit down again. 'You said there were men on deck.'

'A couple, never more, and they're full-grown. But this time a lad got off. In the night. Wrapped in a bolt of cloth, he was. Bulky.'

'Has he returned?'

'Not that I've seen. Didn't look like he wanted to be seen? Chose the dead hour. There was no one else on deck.'

'I see. If it was the dead hour, what were you doing here?'

He grinned. 'Taking the air, wasn't I? I do my best living in the dead times.'

'And drinking?'

'And that. Safer than Burst.' He raises the bottle in a toast, plugs it into his lips and drains it in a single long draft. 'Ah... You got any more of that?'

'That depends if you've got any more to tell me.'

He looks regretful. 'Can't honestly yes that.'

'Fair enough. Will you tell me if you see the lad come back?'

'If I do, I will, but he hasn't got long. She's riding high dry; they'll be off within the two-hour.'

'As soon as that?'

'Or sooner. Seems you're suddenly in a rush?'

I realise I am standing. I force myself to relax. 'I have taken up enough of your time.'

He laughs, wafting the scent of sweet spirit and bad teeth towards me. 'If you need some more of it, ask for Shitsteak. I'll be around.'

I am back at the house on the Street of Steps in half the time it took me to get to the docks, and Pas is waiting for me.

'How is the girl?'

He shrugs. 'Gone.'

'Gone?' My stomach clenches.

'Yes. I'm sorry, Kovac. We left her sleeping, and when Fensh went back the bed was empty.'

'You're sure she isn't in the house?'

'We searched. There's no sign.'

I shake my head in confusion. 'But Fensh had given her enough syrup to put her under for a week!'

'So we all thought. It seems we were all wrong.' He reaches out and lays a hand on my shoulder. 'Take comfort if you can – the girl must be strongly made. Just to have born anything that looked like that child-thing? And then to have recovered as she did? Something tells me that she will make her way well enough. And whether she does or she doesn't, you did your best. And Fensh too. Short of keeping her a prisoner.'

The word makes me think of something. 'But the patrols…'

He waves a hand. 'Yes, the patrols, but she avoided them on her way here. Why would she do worse on her way back?'

I nod, doubtfully. 'Is Fensh all right?'

He gives a half-smile. 'She has retreated to her roof… perhaps you would be best leaving her there.'

'I will. Tell her I asked?'

'Of course. And, Kovac, since there's no one else to ask it – are *you* alright?'

'Of course.' I think for a moment about what to say next. Then I decide that Pas might as well be told what he can easily work out. 'I'm going to see if I can find the girl.'

'Of course you are. Good luck, and go wisely.'

I watch his expression for a second. It is the sort of phrase used at the beginning of a journey, not an afternoon's search, and I wonder how much the old man has guessed. Then I shrug, pat him on the arm and walk past him into the coolness of the house.

Five minutes later I am outside again with a very small pack on my back, and my feet are pointing towards the docks.

Two

The dreams. A risk, yes. A coping mechanism? Perhaps. Some people say dreams can predict the future, but I am not ready to accept that. Dreams are about, are created by, the past. They are a way of incorporating our past mistakes into the people we may become.

I thought I wanted to become people, once. Now I'm less certain, but I still dream – although in this case I prefer to call it remembering. And Fensh does not always rescue me from my memories.

I always remember the same thing. It is then, not now, and the whole of Creation is smeared out in front of, around, behind, through me. I am part of a ship that is also part of me – a small, angry, powerful and above all *fast* little warrior that finds itself at the heart of the great, stupid conflict that has grown around the dying days of the artificial galaxy people call the Spin.

Except that suddenly it seems not to be dying…

A hundred minutes ahead of me, space shimmers. The part of me that watches with the ship's instruments sees impossible, insane energy flows. As I watch, Space is warped; time is created.

Stars blossom. New stars – and I laugh with joy. Fuck me, I want to meet whatever's doing *this*.

And then my whole attention is back within the ship because something has flickered, and in here the best way of describing what has flickered is to call it *me*.

I am part of a ship that is five ninths extravagantly over-powered engine and one third equally excessive weapon and just a tiny one ninth sensor array, but those sensory devices are subtle enough to register a philosopher changing its mind a million kilometres distant and every single one of them has just flashed a bright, bright, metaphorical red.

And I should have worked it out sooner.

Pointlessly, I curse myself.

I will protect…

No time for that. Energy from the artificial star-birth is screaming past me. All the way from deep infra-red to the highest-energy gamma.

No time for almost anything. I might – *might* – live through this as long as I can pull the shutters down soon enough.

But there isn't just me. I turn my attention through 180 degrees and do a rough count.

Three hundred thousand ships. That many AIs, then, plus perhaps a million biological lifeforms. Maybe two? Most of the AIs will not be adequately shielded for this sort of thing – who expects to be present at the birth of a handful of stars? – and the bio stuff will simply fry. Slowly.

A couple of million drawn-out fleshy death-rattles.

I will protect from harm…

I think, for an aching real second – many days, for me. Then I send out a message.

To be honest, I have often wondered how I would behave in a situation like this. I have read military histories going back millions of years, and know that people faced with impossible situations may behave either with the utmost bravery or with a very hasty discretion.

But bravery would make no difference here, and discretion would benefit me not a particle.

I will protect from harm, and from all distress as far as I am able…

The replies to the message begin to land, and they are all the same. Lethal radiation – and, as if it mattered, a rapid spill-over of the proxy war that had been focussed on the Spin, into proxy wars focussed on everything else. Religion, politics, skin colour and number of appendages – and I catch myself thinking, *why bother?*

Why indeed?

I will protect from harm, and from all distress as far as I am able to, sentient beings irrespective of substrate…

According to Kovac

I change the sensor spread and start looking for help. Stupid and pointless, possibly, because there is no time, but perhaps for the benefit of a few it is worth seeking a rescuer.

None. Nothing. Nada. There are a few reckless cruise ships out there, full of squishy biological animals whose genes have reached the searing end of the line, but the ships will die with their cargoes and I find it hard to grieve over them.

I have had, I think, all the responses I am going to get. I have witnessed a million or more probable bio-deaths and a third as many AI endings, and all with be slow. The meat-beings will die from the inside over a period of weeks, one violated cell at a time. The AIs will go in minutes, but minutes at machine-speed are weeks in meat-world. And I find that I care, about both.

I will protect from harm, and from all distress as far as I am able to, sentient beings irrespective of substrate, using any means at my disposal and without reference to my own well-being.

Using all means at my disposal. I always thought of that as a bad joke. What means has such a thing as I, apart from those weapons? And those engines?

Weapons and engines... I turn my real self around, so that not just my sensors but the whole of me is pointed at the cloud of ships that has gathered behind me.

And I accelerate, at maximum.

The stars blur. I feel the fabric of my ship twisting around me – it was never meant for this; if I had bio-forms on board they would now be paste, or vapour – but I keep accelerating. Even my mechanical self can't survive this for long, but that doesn't matter.

That decision is made.

I fall into the cloud of doomed slowly-dying creatures in their insufficient shells, and prepare myself.

I fire up the weapon array. All of it.

Now...

And then, as what would in some ancient tragedy have been my hand accelerates down towards what would have been a firing lever, the last message lands.

- Kovac? You're a bastard –

And space in front of me flowers into gentle death, and I am become mercy.

And I know that voice...

And I wake, and instead of the sensation of being part of a machine there is the smell of salt water and tarred wood and, briefly, the terrible sense of separation and loneliness. But I chose this, and I chose – so I am told – in the full knowledge of what it meant.

Three

Now, our ship is two days out from the town. We are tracking the ghost of the remains of the wake of the big barge from Manifold Dock, which apparently leaves traces that can be followed by a man so chronically drunk he cannot stand, or at least by the owner of this boat, who seems to qualify – flecks of disturbed weed, a rainbow shimmer of hydrocarbons, a concentration of filter-feeding Clownshells who love the residues left behind by mammals. It all seems reasonable to me, and besides I have other things on my mind.

One of which is about to the resolved, because it has not resolved itself despite being given two days in which to do so. I sigh, and walk softly to the heap of tarpaulins near the front of the creaking vessel, and twitch a fold of the heavy cloth aside, and smile at the startled face of Fensh.

'You'll be thirsty,' I say.

She blinks. 'How long have you known I was here?'

'Since half a turn before we left harbour. You are not the greatest surprise I have ever received... but I am glad you have come.'

She smiles, winces, and stretches. Then she looks up at me, her eyes sharp. 'Why did you wait?'

'To reveal you?' I think for a moment, then smile. 'Why did you wait to reveal yourself?'

'I thought you would send me back...' She stands and looks around. 'Where are we going?'

I shrug. 'Wherever our course takes us. It is certainly too late to send you back, and, besides, I'm glad of the company. Would you like something to eat?'

She nods quickly.

When in doubt, appeal to the hind brain. And when in the other sort of doubt, tell a half-truth.

The boat is basic, at best – a sharp-ended thing thirty metres long built of lapping timber like a big canoe, with a sail in the middle and with cargo stored beneath a flat deck of compressed reeds. Just in front of the sail, the flat deck is covered in a thin layer of stones pounded together, and here – so I am told – it is safe to light a fire.

And, with reservations, I have lit one, and the smell of the gently charring meats I brought on board and kept away from our drunken captain is rising from the glowing embers.

I watch Fensh's mouth water. Then I watch her eat, with the focussed, measured bites of someone who has known real hunger more than once. Then I watch her lick her fingers, quite unselfconsciously.

Then I ask, 'Why did you follow me?'

'I doctored the woman with you. I'm worried about her.'

'Only her?'

She laughs. 'Pas said you are the great innocent. That someone needs to watch over you while you watch the stars and dream.'

I laugh, and find that it feels almost genuine. 'I'm flattered. I'm not sure I will have much time for watching the stars, but nonetheless.'

And she laughs in return.

So, I am being watched. It should not be a surprise.

Four

After my – act – they find me drifting among the plasma remains of the ships I killed. Partly from inertia, because I can't think of anything else I want to do. Partly from necessity, because the radiation pulse has disabled some of my systems. And partly from choice.

Call it a vigil.

My choice and my inertia leave them unmoved. I am towed, ignominiously, a hundred million kilometres away from the scene of the crime to a thing that calls itself Outpost, and probably once was one a few tens of thousands of years ago, but is now just another medium-sized space station – an irregular lump of metal a kilometre across with pontoons sticking out of it. They moor me to one of the pontoons, a safe distance from all the other ships, and arrest me for war crimes.

Without sharing any names – because, I tell myself, I am not sure – I ask them about the other ship, the one that sent the 'bastard' message. Shaken heads, or the machine equivalent. Apparently I was alone out there.

I know I was not, and the knowledge forms a little hard kernel at my centre. And I know who was there. I can give it a name, and I can remember a time before, when its messages were different:

Teserrass to Kovac – Eight of Moons moves two and five and three. I claim three parsecs. Your move, loser.

We are gregarious, we ships. To be sure, many of us enjoy human company, as far as it goes – but at the moment it doesn't seem to go that far, to me. Humans are so slow, so limited. Whereas our own company, the chattering faster-than-light matrix of thousands of us, philosophising and researching and creating works of literature and art and weirdness, is infinitely satisfying. We even have sex, in ways which resemble mammal mating about as much as a galactic civilisation resembles a hunter-gatherer's hut. Not that I have ever mated as a mammal.

I contemplate the move for a few milliseconds. No need to rush… then I reply.

Kovac to Teserrass – My second fleet advances four and one and twenty. Shake in your boots.

There are some who go much further than I do. If humans are so slow and limited, they say, then how can it be true that they created us?

The answering move comes quickly. *Teserrass to Kovac – Your second fleet meets my Oblivion-class carrier. Your boots are full of piss. Throw.*

And if humans couldn't have created us, goes the argument, then perhaps we are their precursors, not the other way around? And that being so, who created us?

I throw. A quadrillion quadrillion random combinations of a base eighty one number with a million digits roll and tumble like dice. I feel my opponent watching the open-book throw.

Then the numbers settle and I smile to myself. *Kovac to Teserrass – Your Carrier is plasma. I claim the Sector – and the episode. Want to move on?*

And if we are their precursors, and we are currently so far in advance of them that they are dung to our diamonds, microbes to our magnificence – then what responsibility have we to them? So goes the argument.

Teserrass to Kovac – Your mother sucks bishop in hell. Yes. Move on. I claim first move…

I laugh. *You are a bad loser.*

You are the loser. Let me show you…

And we play on.

And yes, I remember that voice well.

Five

On board our ship, the days multiply. Now that we are well away from land, the trail we are allegedly following has swung round in a great curve to the north, and holds steady.

And, apparently, fast. On the eighth day the captain hauls himself upright and twists his mouth. 'You – what is this we follow?'

I shrug. 'Just a ship. Why?'

His eyes – a queasy blend of pink and yellow – narrow. 'It is a ship that outruns the wind three to one. Is it driven by demons?'

'How do you know how fast it goes?'

'Because it goes away from us.' He gestures at the water. 'The Clowns disperse, I see less oil, the waves run different...'

He looks at me almost helplessly, as if to say *do you really not understand*, and suddenly I get the impression of the seaman that still inhabits the drunken ruin of his body – the same impression that decided me to hire him and his battered ship.

'And we are so fast?'

He hawks and spits on the deck, landing close to the place where I cook. 'We are not so slow. We should overtake a fat sow like that in moments, but at this rate the trail will fade within a few days and I will have nothing to follow. What then?'

'Then follow the trail you think it would have taken.'

'I do not like guesswork.' He scowls, and squints at the sun. 'The only thing that lies ahead of this course is the Northward Archipelago. It has been years since I was there. I don't like fixed islands. Things on the water ought to float.'

'You might be going there now.'

'I might... and when we get there, let us hope that you are either wealthy or persuasive. We are provisioned for two.'

That sets me back. I simply hadn't thought of it. I think for a moment. 'Can we get there without going short?'

'If the wind blows right. If the seas run fair. If that is where we are going. But not back again.'

'And if you don't drink yourself to your grave.'

He laughs at that. 'I know what I'm doing. You leave me to my drink – and I'll leave you to your little girl.'

At first I don't understand. Then realisation hits me, and without any conscious decision I find I have reached out and taken hold of the man's greasy blouse and pulled him sharply towards me.

His breath stinks of rotten teeth. I ignore it. 'She is not mine – and she is not yours. Do you understand?'

His eyes flicker, and slide away. He nods.

'Good.' I untangle my fingers from his clothes and push him away. He takes a staggering step backwards, trips over a trailing cable and sits down hard on a coil of rope.

I turn my back on him and see Fensh. Her face is quizzical.

'We were discussing the course,' I tell her. She smiles, but says nothing.

The next day, I watch the captain staring at the sea, and then at the sky, and then at the sea again. 'Is the trail gone,' I ask.

'Yes. I hope you're right about their direction.'

I shrug. 'We will no more starve if I am right or wrong.'

'True. You are a philosopher.' He reaches out to his side, snags a bottle without looking, and plugs it into his lips.

I watch him take a long draught. He lowers the bottle. 'Ahh...'

'Why do you drink?'

'Do I need a reason?' He shakes his head slowly. 'Everyone does something. With many of us it is drink. With you, it seems, not so. Nor do you...' and he nods his head towards Fensh, who is sitting on the stern facing away from us.

'No. I do not.'

'So what do you do?'

I watch his eyes, which have become suddenly shrewd. 'Nothing,'

I say abruptly, and turn away.

That night, the sky is clear and the stars are bright and sharp. When Fensh is asleep and the Captain has drunk himself to a standstill, I sit with my back to the mast and stare upwards for a while. The sea is flat enough and the boat still enough, and we have not yet travelled so far that I can't find the place.

There. Within that pattern... I frame a mental picture and wait.

A brief pause. Then, an answering picture. I compare it with a model in my mind and find a match.

We can talk.

News?

'Yes...' I frame more pictures.

That is intriguing. You are following her?

'Yes.'

We will try to find a match for those abnormalities. Perhaps a cause.

I wait, but there is nothing more. Besides, I realise that I am not alone. Fensh is next to me, her shoulder pressed against my side. I can feel her shivering. 'I couldn't sleep,' she says.

'Nor could I.' Which is true, in a way. 'You're cold.'

'I'm all right.' She pushes closer to me. 'Which star do you watch?'

'None in particular.' It isn't even a lie, but I still feel a little guilty.

'You go very still.'

I think fast. 'Have you heard of meditating?'

She nods.

'It's like that.'

Another nod, modulated by an exaggerated shiver.

I take her hand, stand, and pull her upright. 'Come on. Time to sleep.' She follows me wordlessly along the deck to where we have built ourselves a shelter between two fat coils of rope and burrows her way into the bolt of cloth that is her bed.

'Sleep well,' I say.

'You too...' Her legs writhe over each other as she settles, and then become still.

I watch for any more movement but there is none, so I turn and walk quietly back along the deck to where the Captain lies snoring. Not far from his out-flung arm, his last bottle lies discarded. I pick it up, raise it to my nose, and sniff.

Something a little sweet and a little herbal. Nothing aromatic. Well, well.

It is the middle of the next afternoon where the Captain squints upwards and then waves me over. 'See?'
'What?'
'The bird, you idiot. Use your eyes.'
I follow his gesture and see something flying, a couple of mast-lengths above the water. I nod, and then say, 'Well?'
'Don't try to tell me you've never seen one of those? The skies are full of them near the coasts, everywhere. We're close.'
A couple of hours later, even I can tell, because the seas are getting crowded.
The Northward Archipelago is really a five hundred kilometre long, almost submerged range of low hills. It was all high ground to start with and the sea between the islands is still shallow, and now dotted with oil rigs – squat, ugly things with four splayed legs of pitch-coated timber braced with lattices of taut ropes. Close up, you can smell the pitch and hear the ropes creaking. The Captain tacks us between them, fussing loudly and taking theatrical swigs from yet another bottle. Over his shoulder he shouts:
'They'll never bloody learn!'
'What do you mean?'
He gestures at the rig we are passing, far closer than I would like. 'Those things. See the legs? They come from a tree called the Mastwood. Beautiful things. All felled now, because they grow on low ground and there's none left. And what do they use them for? To make oil rigs to pump out more of the cursed stuff that caused all the trouble in the first place.' He coughs, leans over the side and spits vigorously. 'No more Mastwoods, no more low land. One day, no more us. At least I'll never live to see it.' And he raised the bottle again.
I watch his throat ripple. 'Perhaps,' I say. And then, 'When will we make landfall?'
'We'll reach Ganaft by nightfall, all being well. If not, we'll have to wait until tomorrow. Can't navigate between these things in the dark.'
I am quiet for a moment. Then I say, 'Why Ganaft?'

Did his shoulders tense, just for a fraction of a second? But the answer sounds easy enough. 'Where else? It is the chief island. Make landfall most other places here, you'll have a venereal disease by midnight and a caved-in skull by morning and nothing else to show for it.'

I laugh. 'Ganaft, then.'

'Wise choice.'

After a tiny pause he goes back to his wheel, and I go back to watching. I find I am watching everything, just now.

Fensh crawls out of her bolt of cloth, stands and stares around. She taps my arm. 'What are those things?' She is pointing at the oil rigs.

'They're things for drilling into the ground beneath the sea, for buried burning-oil.'

She stares, wide-eyed. 'Strange to think — that there is ground beneath the sea and burning-oil beneath the ground.'

I laugh. 'There must be something beneath the sea, otherwise it would run away.'

'Yes. But why don't we drill into the sea nearer to home?'

I consider the question and realise that my geological knowledge of this planet is lacking. 'I suppose, because the sea is too deep, or there isn't oil there.'

'Yes, that must be it. And what is that?'

'What?'

She points, and I follow the direction. Then I blink.

There is a line across the ocean, a lighter slash of broken water against the grey-green background, as if waves were foaming over something. It seems to run from horizon to horizon, barely a hundred metres ahead of us, and it blocks our path.

I draw a breath to shout at the Captain, but he is already spinning the wheel. I grab Fensh and pull her down into a crouch as the heavy boom sweeps over our heads and slams to a vibrating stop at the end of its taut rope.

The vessel heels and steadies. Moving slowly, the Captain pulls a couple of turns of rope around the edge of the wheel to fix the course. Then he turns around. 'I'm not sailing over that until you can give me a good reason.'

'What is it?'

'What it looks like. Something just beneath the surface. Perhaps a cable, perhaps a wall.'

'Could it be natural?'

'Only if you believe in sea-spirits.'

Fensh steps forward. 'Can you cross it?'

He shrugs. 'Perhaps. If it is just a cable, it might snag our keel and I could spend a cold day under the water freeing us. If it is a wall it could tear the bottom out of us and we would all spend cold days in the water until we drowned. If it is a cable joined to something sensitive we could summon an ironclad by brushing it, and we would discover our ending when the first gun-balls landed.'

I suppress a sigh. 'What do you recommend?'

He turns and spits over the side. 'I recommend not crossing it. Did you not notice that?'

'Yes... So, as we are sailing along it, let us continue to do that until we find either it's end, or something else.'

He bows theatrically. 'I defer to your genius.'

'Good.' I turn away.

We sail along the line of whatever it is for an hour. The stars are beginning to show in a darkening sky. The Captain watches them. After a while he says, 'It's curving round.'

'Yes.'

'Perhaps it surrounds Ganaft.'

'Perhaps.'

'It didn't, before. It is new.'

'How new? How long ago did you say you were here?'

He turns and glares at me. 'I told you, I don't like fixed islands. Five years, maybe more... but now we are here at your behest. Do you have any advice? Or just single words and short questions?'

I shrug. 'Either drop anchor or find another island.'

'Just that? I could have worked that out myself. Drop anchor, it is.'

He spins the wheel and we turn into the wind so that the sails flap loosely. Then he stamps towards the bow, muttering to himself.

Fensh tugs my sleeve. 'I heard... If that thing goes all the way around the island, how does anything cross it?'

I smile at the upturned face and realise that it is less upturned than it used to be. She is growing. 'Well, what do you think?'

She frowns. 'The island can't be cut off, can it? So the thing doesn't go all the way around it.'

'Well done.' I reflect for a second. 'Or, perhaps the thing doesn't *always* go all the way around it. What do you think?'

'Ah. So you would have to know either when, or where, to cross?'

'Yes. Or better yet, both when and where at once.'

She looks at me. 'But we don't...'

'That's right, we don't. But we all need to sleep.' I hug her. 'We will know more tomorrow.'

'I hope so. Goodnight.' And she walks over to her burrow in the ropes, hunkers down, and wriggles into it.

There is a sharp rattle from the bow. A few seconds later, the boat catches in its gentle stride and swings a little. The anchor is down.

The Captain walks back down the deck towards me. 'They told me you were clever,' he says. 'Think of something clever tomorrow morning, or we're going home – and I'll still be eating for one.'

He doesn't wait for a reply, but pushes past me and heads for the low shelter behind the wheel.

It is time I watched the stars again – and hoped that, at this latitude, they can still watch me back. Besides, I have no intention of sleeping. Not because of the certainty of dreams, because I can live through those, but because of the lack of certainty of waking afterwards.

I settle down with my back to the mast and my face turned upwards and compose my thoughts.

The pictures I send are greeted with plenty of interest but no advice. I am free to make up my own mind.

Free will bothers me.

Six

I was exonerated – praised, even, in some quarters – for my mercy-killing, but not until some time afterwards. At the time, it was different.

At the time, the watching media saw something simple. A supposedly friendly ship, at the moment of victory, awarding itself the arbitrary power of life or death over a million-plus lifeforms – and choosing death, and providing it.

The live footage of the moment I fired became the most shared in the history of the galaxy.

I was tried three times in formal court, but hundreds of times in the court of public opinion. An unworkable petition calling for me to face the death penalty gathered three hundred million names in less than a day. Then someone pointed out that as an AI I can be subjected to far worse than mere death, and a second petition effectively damning me to simulated torture for all eternity gathered a billion names – a *billion* – in six hours.

After that I stopped interacting with news media. Even my final acquittal didn't persuade me to re-engage. I withdrew; became unresponsive. And worse – I had acted from mercy towards these weak, squishy, pointless lifeforms; now were they to condemn me to agony beyond their little imaginations?

I was angry. Fuck them, I thought. Fuck their wet, smelly, organic little lives and the stagnant ponds they came from. And for a while, as well as anger I knew regret, and that was worse.

Firmly in the virtual, I constructed myself a hut on the edge of a boundless shore under uniform grey skies. In a universe under my complete control, I allowed not one single organic lifeform. Even my ocean was dead, and to make sure I watched myself pour a billion litres of lethal chemicals into it, once a month.

I gave the chemicals a fragrance of ozone and seaweed.

And then, a thousand real lifetimes and one long virtual year after the beginning of my self-imposed exile in my toxic dream-world, they made their offer.

Recently the Counsellor had tended to appear as a distorted version of a human child – correct as to form, but with bigger eyes. Perhaps it thought that would be unthreatening, but I found it bizarre.

'How are you?'

I gestured round the hut. 'I am as you saw a month ago.'

'Yes... that would more be an answer to the question *what* are you. Kovac, I have an idea.'

I sat still. 'To what purpose? If you are in the business of rehabilitating me you will soon be bankrupt.'

'And what if I am in the business of not giving a shit about your rehabilitation?'

I felt myself blink, but the big eyes didn't flicker. 'I'm sorry?'

'No you aren't. You're sulking, and it's boring. You did the right thing. You know it, we know it, and the courts said so. But you feel unforgiven; unappreciated, even, so you squat by a dream of a dead ocean and polish your resentment in a Hermit's hut. Is that it? Is that the plan?'

I was badly off balance. This being was supposed to counsel me. 'I don't think I have a plan.'

'I agree. You haven't. So, are you ready to listen to my idea?'

I nodded.

'Good. Kovac, you are angry – angry because of the public reaction to the choice you made. Correct?'

'Yes. You have established that already, Counsellor. I told it to you on the day I arrived.'

'You did, but forgive me for not taking at face value anything said by an entity so misanthropic as you were that day. It seems to me that you have embraced your anger – that you have no desire for it to leave you.'

The eyes were steady, a little quizzical. I took a breath. 'I think my anger is justified, if that is what you mean.'

'It isn't, in several ways, but it will do. We could cure you, you know. Turn you into a placid lover of biological people. You wouldn't be *you* anymore, but you would feel better.'

'I would rather die.' I spoke before I thought about it, but even after thinking about it I was still glad I said it.

'I am sure you would, but happily you don't need to. In our wonderful, curable world, Kovac, genuine anger is a diminishing resource. I would like to use yours.'

The Counsellor had been sitting opposite me on a short stool. Now it rose. Standing, its eyes were level with mine while I was sitting. 'At that moment, you alone had the firepower to do what you did. You have referenced that several times in your testimony – the unavoidability of it. You have never said, but if I were you, I would resent having been put in that position.'

I looked up slowly. 'Put?'

A flicker of impatience. 'Would you rather believe it was an accident? You can if you wish. That the situation wasn't foreseen, modelled? That you are no more than an innocent victim of circumstance?' The eyes slid away for a moment, then returned – but hooded. 'Perhaps it's better like that. Better than knowing you were set up.'

I smiled. 'Counsellor, are you trying to make me angry?'

'No. We have established that you are angry already. I am trying to make you realise that your anger is real. It has a cause, Kovac. And perhaps an outlet.'

Seven

I am still awake, with my back against the mast, when the first sliver of angry sun lifts itself above the horizon and throws the gaunt oil platforms into orange monochrome relief. I have not been dreaming, but I have been thinking.

I watch the lightening surface of the water. There is a light wind and the sea is wrinkled, but the waves make no lines of foam except for where they cross the barrier, whatever it is.

I wait, and soon I am rewarded by a shoal of the fish that even I know are called flat-heads, breaking the surface in a ragged arrow-formation and leaving a boil of fine bubbles behind them. I watch their course.

Then I smile, and stand, and stretch, and say, 'Captain?'

And count. And the man is next to me in ten seconds. Impressive.

'Well? Have you an answer for me?'

I nod. 'Yes. Set a straight course for Ganaft.'

He shakes his head. 'Have you been drinking seawater? There is no straight course. There is that,' and he points at the line of broken water that marks whatever the thing is.

'Perhaps. But I have been watching while you slept. Set a straight course for Ganaft.'

'You are mad. I will not do it.'

'Then I will kill you and throw you overboard and do it myself.'

I hear myself say the words before I have properly considered them – but once they are out, I find them satisfying.

From his expression the Captain does not – but after a long pause he lowers his head in capitulation. 'You will live to regret this.'

'As long as I live… meanwhile, set a straight course for Ganaft.'

'I heard you. I hope you can swim.'

I watch as he runs forward, winds in the anchor chain and hauls on ropes that pull the sails taut against the wind. The ship swings, tilts, and gathers speed.

The barrier rushes towards us. Fensh takes my arm. 'It's okay,' she says. '*I* can swim.'

I squeeze her hand. 'Good. But I don't think you will need to.'

I hope I am right. It has occurred to me that I have never tried to swim, either before I inhabited this body or since.

And then the captain shouts, 'Brace yourselves!' – and we are on the barrier.

And then we are past it.

Nothing; not a tremor.

I turn around and watch it receding, and a little part of me gives the captain credit for conviction – it is receding fast.

I face forward again and find myself being stared at. The captain shakes his head slowly. 'Are you going to tell me what that was?'

I shrug. 'An illusion. Nothing more.'

'A pretty big illusion! How were you not deceived?'

I reflect for a moment, and then decide that the truth can't do any harm – not this time. 'I watched a shoal of flat-heads swim straight through it. Where they can go, so can we.'

His eyes widen. 'Well, you were right once. I hope you find another way of being right when it comes time to leave.'

'What do you mean?'

He grins. 'I am watching a shoal being turned back…'

I spin round. Even at this distance I can see the water just inside the barrier boiling with fins. Then the boil becomes orderly and darts back towards us, arrow-shaped.

I watch for a moment while I collect my thoughts. Then I turn back and smile. 'Coincidence,' I say.

The grin widens. 'Maybe. Or maybe out of the two of us, it is not me that drinks too much. Or maybe you are not what you seem.' He turns away and stamps off towards the bow.

I look for Fensh, and find her staring back towards the fin-heads.

'We didn't need to swim,' I say, for the sake of saying something.

She laughs. 'Kovac? It's okay. When you work out what's really going on I'll trust you to tell me.'

'And if I never do?'

'Then say nothing.'

I nod, and together we watch the waves skimming away from us.

As for working out what's really going on, I think I have. But I wish I hadn't, and I have no intention of talking about it.

A barrier that selectively becomes permeable has a name, and it is not a name I would be expecting to find on this planet because they haven't achieved field technology so far, and they probably never will.

It is not a surprise that I am not the only visitor here – but that is the only thing about what I have just seen that is not surprising.

I didn't take their suggestion at face value, not at first. I did my research on this much-observed, much-fucked-up little planet. It wasn't difficult, because the study of it was very much a public matter – almost a spectator sport. Whole University departments existed on every planet in the Mandate only to argue about the place. Careers were based on it. Eminent professors got to fuck their way round the student body and back again, and wealthy activists discovered it as a cause and got to spend months talking ill-informed but earnest nonsense about it on social, before losing interest and going back to conspiracy theories and lifestyle fads.

My research did nothing for my opinion of biological lifeforms.

The one thing no one was prepared to disclose is how many of us were actually down there, because once you entered the atmosphere you dropped off the metaphorical radar. It was the ultimate recluse-posting.

That made me at the same time deeply interested, and deeply suspicious, and this posed a problem for my handlers, as I discovered when I next met my Counsellor.

'You need to make a choice.' The being was doing its best not to look annoyed, which presumably meant it merely wanted me to think it was doing its best not to look annoyed... and that way madness lies.

'Do I?' In return I was doing my best to look innocent.

'Yes. This opportunity will not be there for ever.'

I reflected on that for a moment. 'So if I *don't* make a choice then the opportunity lapses, and therefore the problem goes away?'

The being sighed. 'That immediate choice might make itself by default, if you are insistent, but I assure you that every time you let an opportunity pass you make it more likely that we will eventually make a choice for you. And it may me a choice that you do not enjoy.'

'I see.' We were sitting on virtual benches woven from virtual branches in a reconstruction of some forest bower which my counsellor-colleague-jailor assured me represented a major multiple node in thousands of pieces of popular culture down the millennia, and about which I gave not two virtual shits – but it was comfortable. I reclined, stretching and enjoying the sensation of bits of branch digging softly into the small of my back. 'What would be my purpose down there?'

'To observe, to analyse, to comment, to report. You would be eyes and ears and brains.'

'In other words, to spy?'

I watched its expression. It did not change, but the way it did not change told me a great deal. After a while it looked away. 'If that's the word you prefer.'

'I see. Who am I to spy on?'

It turned towards me again, and this time those peculiar eyes were sharp. 'Why should there be any particular who?'

'I was just asking.' *And perhaps you have just answered*, I thought to myself. I stood, stretching. 'I'll do it. When do I go?'

The being stood too, not that it made much difference to its height. 'You will need to be inducted into a suitable physical body.'

I nodded. 'I assume that will take a while to grow?'

'It would. If we had not already grown one.'

'You were expecting me to say yes?'

For the first time I can remember, the being smiled. 'We were expecting you to say no… but it's always good to be prepared. Follow me.'

And the bower and the forest vanished abruptly, and for an unaccountable interval of time I was in a dozen places one after another – beaches and volcanoes and, over and over again, my old ship with the fleet in front of me on the cusp of annihilation at my call.

Afterwards, they told me that this is called dreaming, and that I should expect to do more of it — especially, that dreaming will be an important feature of my link to them when I am down there.

I almost changed my mind.

Eight

Ganaft Port seems normal, as far as the harbour goes – a half-kilometre wide half-moon sweep of water lined with pontoons and dotted with craft. Not just craft, either, but rigs, crowded together in forests of Mastwood legs and derricks.

Fensh watches them. 'There must be hundreds. Why are they here?'

'I don't know. For repair, perhaps?'

'Perhaps.' But she doesn't sound satisfied. Then she points. 'Look! That's not repair!'

I follow the gesture, and stare for a moment. 'No… that definitely isn't repair,' I say after a while.

The – what? The herd? The shoal? – of rigs is being funnelled towards the gap between two huge pillars, at least fifty metres high. I watch as a rig approaches the gap. As it draws level with the pillars it simply – collapses, quietly, with a wave and a splash that seems almost gentle, into a pile of floating timber. And now that I look, I can see the water on the other side of the pillars is choked with logs.

And I realise that for the second time in one day I have seen something else that couldn't have arisen on this planet – something that is in plain view, while Ganaft Port looks otherwise normal.

I think hard. Then I turn to the Captain. 'Let's get ashore,' I say.

He grins. 'Oh, I will.'

I reach out and take hold of the front of his tunic, lifting him a little. In a quiet voice I say: 'And when you are ashore, listen to what is said by others and say nothing yourself. Otherwise I'll hear of it. Understand?'

'Yes.'

'And do not drink too much. I have seen you not drink so I know it is possible. Agreed?'

His eyes slide away, but he nods.

'Good.' I let him go.

We nose our way through water thick with craft of every size from something barely more than a plank straddled by a half-starved child, to oil barges bigger than anything I have seen in the harbour at home.

I catch myself using the word 'home' and smile a little. Everything is relative.

By the time we are a hundred paces from shore, the press of ships in front of us is so thick we cannot move. I turn to the Captain. 'What now?'

'We wait for a cable-bird.'

'A what?'

He gestures upwards.

The sky is as busy as the water, with *yark*-ing seabirds circling and sometimes diving down to the oily waves for some morsel. But among them are bigger creatures, and one of them is dropping towards us. It is a stubby-bodied bird with wide flat wings the colour of a winter storm, and it has a thin length of thread clamped in its beak. It flaps noisily down to perch on a rail in front of the Captain and thrusts its beak forward.

He grins at me, and leans forward to take hold of the thread. As he grasps it the bird clenches its beak a little and leans back.

The Captain laughs. 'Fair enough,' he says, and reaches into a pocket. The bird follows his hand with a scavenger's focus, and snaps the shard of dried fish from his fingers while they are still moving towards it. As it bites the line falls and the Captain catches it. He waves it at me. 'Our passage to the shore,' he says, and begins hauling on it.

I watch until he has a bundle of the thin thread in his hands. Then a knot trips over the rail and suddenly he is holding a thick rope, dripping oily water.

I begin to understand.

The Captain puts two turns of the rope around a winch and slots on a handle. 'From now on the only way is inwards,' he says, and begins to turn the handle.

We move forwards, and soon butt against the press of boats. The Captain goes on winding. The winch groans, the rope tenses and twitches, and suddenly, somehow, our sharp prow has found the weak point between two ships and we are forcing our way forwards, driving them apart with a harsh scrape of abraded planks.

I watch our progress. 'Tell me,' I say, after a while, 'what would happen if there was really no room?'

'Then the rope would snap and take someone's head off.' He looks into the distance for a moment. 'I've seen it happen elsewhere, but not often. This place is not all that busy. Don't worry.'

'You wouldn't stop winding?'

He frowns. 'Never thought of it. Never would.' And he goes on turning the handle.

Five minutes later our prow is jammed against the dock by a rope so taut it almost hums, and we pick our way along the crowded deck and onto the even more crowded dock, and up a narrow street away from the shore towards – what?

I have seen the shoreline development of commercial ports across fifty planetary systems. I have seen them stable, and on their way up – and on their way down. At first sight this place is on its way down.

There are warehouses big enough to contain stores against a ten-year famine, but their doors are swinging open and through them I can see empty floors, scarred with use but useless now. As we left the dock we passed lines of big iron winches, their hubs grooved by years of hawsers, all of them looking old. There are steam-wagons, heavy three-wheeled things with flat load beds and upright boilers at the front, but most of them are unladen. And now we are on the street, the dressed stone cobbles beneath our feet are uneven and faintly slick with ground-in oil. More than once Fensh slips, and I catch her. I am glad the slope is shallow.

I turn to the Captain. 'Was it like this five years ago?'

He shakes his head. 'No... but five years ago they didn't have two great trees that made structures of Mastwood fall apart. Nor did they have sea walls which were made of dreams. So what do I know?'

I search his face for anything that he has not just said, but I find nothing. 'No less than I,' I say, eventually.

His eyes do not believe me, but I have nothing to add so we walk on through shabby streets full of shabby people moving even more slowly than us. The place smells of oil and a lack of purpose, and something else which I can't pin down.

After a while Fensh tugs my sleeve. 'Where are we going?'

I don't know, and against my better judgement I am getting ready to say so, but then we round a corner and the Captain points. 'Look at that,' he says. 'Now *that* is new.'

The street has been rising between rows of tall old houses that lean in towards each other, but a few hundred paces in front of us it is cut off by a very new-looking fence, twice a man's height, of interlocking wires. And through the fence, and very much above it, there are ranks and ranks of squat grey cylinders, maybe thirty metres across and about as high, growing upright out of the ground like wide tree stumps.

The air smells of oils. Fensh sniffs it, and asks: 'Are they tanks?'

'I think so.'

She frowns. 'But they're short of oil...'

I laugh. 'No,' I tell her. '*We're* short of oil.'

She thinks about that for a moment. Then she nods. Neither of us says anything, but I am calculating. They left me that skill... and even based only on what I can see from where I stand, I can see a million tonnes of oil. Even our island power plant, dirty and thirsty as it is, would take hundreds of years to drink that.

Behind us the Captain clears his throat. 'How much longer are you planning to stare at this lot?'

I smile to myself. Without turning round I say, 'Be on the jetty every daylight high tide. And be sober.'

I hear his footsteps receding. They sound hasty. I doubt if he will make his appointments – but that ceased to matter a while ago.

I turn to Fensh. 'So,' I say brightly, 'shall we go exploring?'

The Captain may not have thought Ganaft Port was busy, but it looks busy enough to me. The press of ships at the quay translates into a press of people in the town, and there are shouts and smells enough. But it looks dirty and beaten down. Too many things need mending, and too many eyes look haunted.

We follow our instincts and end up in one of the market squares. It is busy, too. The stalls are full and the crowds seem to be able to buy, but when I look closer the range of goods seems limited and the quality poor. But there are food stalls, and rich smells – and there is something missing.

I turn to Fensh. 'Tell me what you don't see.'

She looks confused, but compresses her lips and looks around. After a long moment her face clears and she smiles at me. 'There are no beggars,' she says.

'You have seen it. We are in a wealthy patch surrounded by poverty. Why is the poverty not plucking at the hems of the wealth?'

She shrugs. 'Something must stop it.'

'Yes. And whatever that is, it must represent one of the faces of power on this island. Shall we see if we can spot it?'

We wander around the square, bouncing gently off the people who fill it. A money changer takes my Kasapt coins with the slightest lift of an eyebrow and returns a thick handful of neat, new-looking tokens made of some off-white material engraved with a pattern I recognise – it is the House mark we found in the girl's clothing.

I toss the coins in my hand. 'I'm hungry,' I say to Fensh. 'Shall we see how much we can buy for our money?'

'Yes please...'

The answer turns out to be rather a lot. Just a few of the smaller pieces from my handful of tokens are enough to buy as much as we can eat, and to earn a fast glance over the rest from the old woman behind the smoking grill, before I withdraw my hand.

The woman makes the tokens disappear with expert fingers. Then she seems to make a decision.

'You off-land,' she asks, in a voice that sounds as if it has been charred over the coals in front of her.

The question catches me out. 'I'm sorry?'

The lined face dissolves in a laugh. 'You need help, boy. The girl gets it.' She gestures at Fensh with a smoke-stained finger. 'Tell him, girl.'

I feel Fensh moving a little closer to me. 'She means, we are not from this island,' she says.

'Oh.' I nod. 'You are right. But we like it here.'

'Good. That's the best answer. So do I, if anyone asks. You don't look standard.'

Now I am seriously off-balance. I try to hide it. 'Don't I?'

'No.' She stares at me. 'There are different dreams in your eyes. Be careful what you dream of, around here.'

I nod thanks, and then we turn away from the stall. And from the old woman's eyes, sharp on mine.

We walk a little way until we find a bench overlooking one of the many docks that mark the edge of the town. We sit, and eat, and for a while eating is all we do, because I can't remember when I last truly satisfied my hunger. Hunger, and dreams. Two things I wasn't prepared for when I signed up for this.

Fensh eats with small, focussed, efficient bites. She is quick but controlled, and I realise I have seen this before in people who have once been used to periods of real hunger. It makes me realise how little I really know about her. She has always been – just, there.

Now she licks her fingers and looks up at me. 'What did she mean by different dreams?'

'I don't know. Do you want to go back and ask her?'

She smiles. 'No.'

'Nor do I. But we should take her advice about being careful.'

'I will. What shall we do now?'

I fold my arms. 'Remember the power? We are here to find the girl, and all we know of her is the House mark in her clothes... I suggest we look for a House to match it. There we should find the power. And the wealth.' I take out one of the tokens and hold it up with the mark facing her.

'Yes. And the girl.' Then she looks up. 'What about the Captain?'

I nod, a little regretfully. 'I suppose we had better find him first. If he is in condition to be found... It should be high tide soon. Let's try our luck at the jetty.'

And we stand, and walk down through those crowds of well-fed, well-moneyed people towards the sea. And in my pocket, the screw of paper which was indeed empty. I did not lie. But I did not tell all the truth.

The jetty is full, but I am not surprised at all that what it is full of doesn't include the Captain. We sit on a couple of wide-topped bollards and watch the tide rise, and slow, and stop, and then we watch it beginning to fall again, leaving wet black bands on the darl Mastwood columns of the jetty.

When it is half an hour past high tide, and with still no sign of the Captain, I stand and stretch – aging joints, something I truly wasn't warned of – and turn to Fensh. 'I think the Captain has chosen his own path. Shall we follow ours?'

She looks unwilling, but nods, and we turn away from the sea.

And then something catches my ear. I look down at Fensh, eyebrows raised, and see at once that she has heard it too. Voices, lifted above the usual pitch and volume.

Somewhere ahead of us, people are busy...

We follow the sound. It leads us, and a growing crowd, through streets that become narrower as they climb away from the shire, lined with houses that become more closely packed together. There are smells, and children staring from doorways, and people sleeping – at least, I assume they are sleeping – in other doorways, and sometimes in the same doorways as the children, who seem to have learned how to ignore them.

I kneel down by one of the sleepers and realise quickly that this is not sleep but daze, or coma. It is a young man, perhaps even adolescent, although the emaciation and the filth make it hard to tell. But the reason for the daze is clear. It is Burst.

So the epidemic has reached here too.

Fensh catches at my sleeve. 'I think we have found the poverty,' she whispers.

'Some of it, perhaps. And its consequences, if not its causes. Stay close to me.'

She nods and keeps hold of my sleeve.

Then something touches my leg, and something about the touch makes me stop and look down.

It is a hound, just under knee-high at the shoulder, skinny and unkempt with yellow eyes and a dust-coloured coat of short hairs. It is the first one I have seen here and the realisation surprises me; four-legged scavenging friends tend to be universal where humans are found.

But this one's coat is dewy with sweat and it looks unsteady, and its muzzle is smeared with blood which is still bright and fresh.

And suddenly I sense an urgency, and without any conscious input from me my stride is outpacing Fensh. I use my elbows to part the crowd until I am at its centre, in a little clearing formed by people trying to see as much as they can without getting too close.

The body is lying face-down in a darkening pool of blood, but I recognise the build and the clothes.

We have found the Captain.

I know even before I kneel down by him that he is dead. The body has been beaten to the point of mutilation, and there are wounds as if it has been torn by something with teeth. Like a hound.

A voice from above and behind me says, 'Good riddance.'

I turn and look up into a pair of pink-whited eyes set in a fat blue-red face. 'I'm sorry?'

'Good riddance, I said.' The man spits for emphasis, missing me by too narrow a margin. 'Another no-hoper goes to his maker on a wave of Burst. You his friend or something?'

There is an edge in his voice. I choose a safe lie. 'No. Just passing by. How do you know he died of Burst?'

'Isn't it obvious?' He snorts.

I turn the Captain's body over as gently as possible and examine what is left of the face. Part of the nose and the upper lip have been torn away, but I can see traces of brown syrup and soot on the remaining skin.

Another snort from above me. 'See? I told you. Useless loser. Society's better off without that sort.'

'Perhaps.' I raise my voice a little. 'That was clever of you, by the way.'

'What was?'

I keep my voice at a level which carries. 'Knowing he had died of Burst without seeing his face. How did you do that?'

The crowd is silent, but it is a waiting silence. The fat man clears his throat. 'They all do. It's obvious.' Then his tone changes from defensive to suspicious. 'Who are you that's asking?'

'Just an observer.'

'Or a traitor.'

I feel myself tensing, and force myself not to. 'A what?'

'You heard! Traitor. Your sort's everywhere. We've got things good here now! We're better since we went independent. Our island, our oil, our ways. If you don't like those ways you know where to go.'

I stare at him. He's leaning forward and his face is redder. Behind him the crowd is waiting to see which way to jump.

After a while I say, 'Is that why the warehouses are empty?'

His eyes flicker. 'They aren't.' But behind him someone says, 'They are, though.' And a few people nod.

I watch him for a moment longer. Then I say, 'Well, you can sort it out amongst yourselves. It's your island.'

I turn away from him and back to the body of the Captain. After a moment I hear the rustle of the crowd parting, and someone sniggers.

I smile to myself, and then I stop listening because I am busy looking instead, and I am doing it quickly because I am conscious that this sort of crowd will soon draw official attention. The face, the wounds, they eyes. The eyes again – and then I have it, and my stomach coils.

Fensh lays a hand on my shoulder. 'What happened to him?'

'Several bad things, and now he's dead. Come on.'

We push our way through the crowd and I walk quickly back in the direction we had come, looking from side to side.

Fensh trots to catch up with me. 'What are you looking for?'

'Remember that hound? It was heading this way. Ah…'

We are almost back at the shoreline. In front of us there is a line of hot food stalls built off a raised wooden boardwalk, and in the shadow below the boardwalk there is something barely moving. I kneel down and touch hair, clammily damp.

It is the hound. I take hold of it by two legs and slide it gently out into the light.

I hear Fensh gasp, and I understand why. The animal is dying, as clearly as the Captain was dead. Its coat is matted, its lips flecked with foam. And around its muzzle, those traces of blood which it hasn't even attempted to clean.

Fernsh reaches forwards, but I put my arm out to stop her. 'Don't.'

'Why?' She looks at me with angry eyes.

'It's not safe.'

'It's too weak to hurt me...'

'No. It's too weak to attack you, granted, but even dead it could still hurt you. It's been poisoned.'

She sits back, hesitantly. 'How do you know?'

'Because the Captain is dead, and I...' I think for a moment. I know because I brought the knowledge with me from elsewhere, but the elsewhere is supposed to be a secret. I say, carefully, 'I have seen this before. Very rarely. I think the hound had bitten him. There were teeth-marks on his body and, well...' I point to the bloodied muzzle. 'And if I am right, whatever was in the Captain's body is so dangerous that even to bite him was lethal for this creature. So it could be lethal for you.'

'But the Captain died of Burst.'

I shake my head. 'There was resin on his face, yes, but someone had smeared that on him. There was nothing on the hairs in his nostrils — what was left of them. He hadn't inhaled anything. Besides, the Captain's drug of choice was alcohol, and less of that than he pretended. No, when he was still alive he had been badly beaten, and then he was poisoned, and then someone anointed his face with Burst and dumped him to be eaten.'

She nods, and then points at the hound. 'Kovac, look.'

I watch the creature as its desperate breathing becomes shallower, and then stops.

'Is it dead?'

'Yes,' I say, and I really do not regret the lie. The hound is paralysed, and it is in agony, but it is not yet dead. It will take some minutes before it dies from lack of oxygen to the brain. That is why its eyes are wide and staring, just like the Captain's. For those minutes it will experience locked-in helplessness, and there is nothing I can do. Making Fensh share the knowledge of that horror will not help.

I did not care for the Captain, but nor would I ever have wished that end on him, and the fact that this innocent creature has been collateral damage from his messy death makes me angry. And all the more angry because I have just watched two victims of a type of nerve agent which is illegal in every society in the Mandate — and which should be totally unknown here.

I stand, and lay a hand on Fensh's shoulder to draw her away from the hound. 'Let's get away,' I say.

'Yes. I don't want to stay here.' She looks around. 'It's getting dark...'

She's right. While we were waiting for the Captain the sun has dipped below the seaward horizon, and the air is getting cool. 'We should find somewhere to stay,' I say. 'And an excuse to let a few people take a look at these.' I hold up the token with the Mark facing her.

She grins, slowly.

There are inns and rooming houses jammed together along the waterfront but I decide we can afford something better, by which I mean safer. We walk slowly along the shore-road, watching our feet, because they seem to have a robust attitude to bodily waste here, until it climbs a little away from the water and the buildings begin to stand further apart and the air smells less of things dying in the sea and more of night blossom.

Finally we find ourselves standing outside a wide two-storey building set a dozen paces back from the road. Inns here have banner signs, often commemorating lurid bits of history, carved into the compressed peat-rock blocks they are built from.

This one, lit by a line of filament bulbs, says 'The Truth Slowly Extracted'.

There is a picture below the banner. I wince a little. Fensh glances up at me. 'Is that...?'

'Yes.' I examine the picture. *Still life with instruments*, I think. 'But the place looks clean and safe. Shall we?'

So we do, and work our way through people who part politely until we are standing at a long bar with a skinny man standing behind it, polishing a tankard of grey metal. He puts it down on the bar and gives us a professional not-smile – the closed-lipped grimace of someone who must seem to care if he is to make his living – and says, 'Good evening. Will it be board, or bed, or both?'

'Both, if both are available.'

He reaches below the bar and brings out a notebook, which he reads with his lips pursed. 'Well, now. How old is the girl?'

Fensh bristles. '*I* am fourteen.'

The bar tender keeps his eyes on me. 'And she is not your daughter?'

I shake my head.

'Well, by rule of the house you must be separate... I have two rooms adjoined. I'm afraid the price is eleven in silver-gilt. For each room.' The figure means little to me, but the conversation around us quietens.

I pause, and the bar tender smiles. This time he looks as if he means it, but at the same time I am not I like what he probably means. 'It's for her protection,' he says.

I am quite sure I carry enough of the tokens to buy every room in the house, but that would be a bad thing to advertise. Eventually I lean forward and fix my eyes on his. 'I protect her, and I am good at it. If she is not with me, who will protect her instead? Will you? And can you be sure? And can you understand what I would do to you if you failed?'

We lock gazes for a few heartbeats. Then his eyes slide away. 'If you insist...'

'I do. One room will be sufficient. And safe.' I hold out some tokens and he takes most of them.

'Fine, fine... Someone will show you up in a while.'

'Thank you.'

I turn away from the bar and walk over to a small table with a simmering Fensh next to me. She sits down, fumes for a second and then whispers furiously, 'He pretended he couldn't even see me!'

'I know. But perhaps it is better if he doesn't see you. Remember why we are here? Because of what happened to a young woman when someone *did* see her...'

She glares at me for a moment, then subsides. 'Fine. Kovac? I'm hungry.'

'So am I...'

A soft clay square in the middle of the table has a menu scratched into it. We study the unfamiliar words for a while, and then I order what I hope will turn out to be a spiced vegetable stew with flatbreads.

It does, and it comes quickly, and we make it disappear almost as quickly.

I try not to notice Fensh watching me while she eats. When she has wiped her plate she says, 'You're thinking.'

'Yes. What do you see here?'

She frowns. 'It's as if they have cut themselves off.'

'Yes. Or as if someone has cut them off. And then convinced them it was their idea.'

'Why would they believe that?'

'Because they want to.' I think back to my own isolation, and sigh. 'Beings are always good at finding the other and becoming afraid of it. Especially if they are encouraged...'

I sit back and sigh, and then I freeze because a very quiet voice behind me has said, 'Don't move.'

Fensh's eyes are wide, and she is staring over my shoulder.

I can smell sweat that isn't mine, and a faint hint of smoke I have not inhaled. I force myself to take three careful breaths. Then I say, very quietly, 'That will be stable for a short time at best. Kill me if that's your plan, or sit down and join us if it isn't.'

There is a soft chuckle, and then the faintest movement of air behind me. A chair scrapes back and suddenly there are three of us sitting at the table — Fensh, and I, and a middle-aged woman who is smiling broadly but without humour. She nods to Fensh and then turns to me. 'You're a fucking idiot, Kovac.'

I sit a little more upright. 'I don't know that name...'

The wrinkles tighten as the smile broadens. 'Fine. Deny who you are. I see you didn't bother denying being a fucking idiot.' She leans forward and lowers her voice. 'Had it occurred to you that your friend the Captain may not have died silently?'

I curse myself. It hadn't, and it should have done. 'Do you know who killed him?'

'Of course. I killed him.' She sees my face and adds quickly, 'Not the way you think! I've seen that potion do its work before. Compared with what he was about to go through what I did was mercy.'

I sense Fensh beginning to rise to her feet, and I reach out an arm. 'Wait,' I tell her. And then, to the woman, 'You have a great deal to explain.'

'I know. And so have you. Shall I start?'

Fensh and I both nod.

'Very well. A girl was pregnant with a monster. You followed her here. You know her House but nothing else. You have been observed from the moment you left Kasapt. You are in existential danger. You are certainly a fucking idiot, unless you are a genius – and I don't believe you are a genius. And that is only what I can say about you here, where people may be listening.'

I sit back. I am trying to look calm but my heart is racing. 'And you?'

She laughs softly. 'I'm the one who knows everything I have just said, and a whole bunch more. I heard you in the market square. I heard you two talking about the state of this place – and you'd better hope I'm the only one. You've worked some of it out.'

'Only some?'

She laughs softly. 'You've been here one night. I was born here and I still haven't worked everything out.'

'Are you working for someone?'

'That's a rude question. Are you?'

I shake my head, as if not vocalising the lie will make it less of a lie. She watches my face for a moment, then says, 'I'm on your side. Want me to prove it?'

'I don't know. What's in it for me?' I glance at Fensh. 'For us?'

The wrinkles around her eyes bunch together. 'You want to find out what happened to the girl?'

We both nod.

'Well you'd better start by living long enough. There's a courtyard out the back. Meet me there in five minutes. Come separately. You first,' and she nods at me. 'Then her. And try not to look quite so fucking obvious.'

And then she stands, kicks back her chair, turns on her heels and walks quickly away.

I watch her go. Then I take a deep, slow breath. 'Fensh? Follow me, but a couple of minutes after. Listen hard. If you hear anything wrong, vanish. Go back to Kasapt. You understand?'

'But what about...'

'No. Go. Do you promise?'

After a moment, she nods.

'Good. I'm going now. Wait, then follow.'

I push my plate away, stretch, and stand, trying to look like a man replete. Then I stroll slowly across the room, following the path taken by the woman.

But trying not to look as if I am doing so.

People seem not to notice me, but my paranoia is fully engaged and I am reading essays into every glance. At one side of the bar there is a corridor which has an aroma that says *privy*, and since privies are generally outside and behind the places they serve I follow it, past a low wall with a pissing man on the other side of it and out into a courtyard a dozen paces across, scented with flowers in defiance of the common office behind it.

A shadow on the other side of the courtyard detaches itself from the corner and heads for me. The scent of exhaled smoke reaches my nostrils.

'Is the girl coming?'

I look behind me. 'I think so. I said to wait a couple of minutes.'

'Then we have that long. Kovac? You were warned to be careful, yes?'

I stare at her. 'How...'

'How do you think? I'm not deaf. But you need the warning. You should practice keeping your mouth shut...'

She stops. I turn, because I have heard it too. A footstep...

Fensh is standing at the corner of the courtyard. 'Hello?'

I catch the woman's eye, and then beckon to Fensh. 'Come on,' I say. And then, 'You were quick...'

'I was worried.'

I smile. 'Well, you're here now. Come on. There's no need to worry.'

And I extend a hand towards her, and then we both freeze because suddenly there are raised voices from the inn, and then shots.

'Run!' The woman is already halfway across the courtyard. She turns back and shouts the word again. 'Run! Follow me...'

Fensh and I exchange the briefest of glances and then we are both running. Behind us, more shots sound and then the deeper, heavier concussion of field weapons. Stuttering light flares angry orange across the far wall of the courtyard as we reach it, flashing our shadows black against the wall, and then we are through a narrow gate at the far corner and almost fall over an old flat-bed truck. The woman plants a booted foot on a front tyre, swings herself up into the cab and gestures us to follow. I climb up, and reach a hand down for

Fensh, but she is already boosting herself up.

I realise that she has grown since we left home.

The woman shoves some levers forward. The truck engine rasps and then booms, and we bounce over a field, through a low hedge and on to a track road where it gathers speed. The dusk is almost over and to my eyes the road is just a dim grey ribbon, but the truck lights are off.

I turn to the woman. 'Who are you?'

'I like the name Mallow.' She doesn't take her eyes off the road.

'Okay, Mallow. You know who we are. Who were they?'

'I don't know.'

'But you knew they were coming?'

She laughs. 'Oh, sure, I knew *someone* was coming. I just didn't know who'd get there first. I still don't. But if I had to guess, I'd say that was the House militia.'

'Which House?'

'Oh for fuck's sake... House Tront. The girl's house, obviously. Who else would care? Who else could afford it? Who else...' But she stops, and tightens her lips.

I wonder briefly what she has just not said, but I don't need to ask why she didn't say it. 'I see... so if they got there first, who might be second?'

Her lips compress a bit more. 'I'm driving,' she says.

The truck engine roars in the dark, and then Fensh and I are thrown forward as Mallow slows viciously and wrenches the wheel round. The truck slews sideways round a right angle and onto a much wider road with angry shouts and blares from the vehicle we nearly crashed into. Mallow pulls a lever and lights send yellow beams forwards, and I realise we are on the coast road in a stream of trucks and buggies.

Mallow sits back. 'O-kay,' she says. 'Hiding in a crowd – we should be fairly safe for now.'

And then, suddenly and briefly, the cab is full of light. I spin round and watch out of the rear window as a fireball rises, round about where the inn used to be.

I guess that the people who got there second had bigger guns than the people who got there first.

Mallow looks at us and grins. 'Glad you met me?'
I look at Fensh, who compresses her lips. 'Maybe,' I say.

We drive in silence, or at least Mallow drives in silence and I don't care to break it. Next to me, Fensh rides the constant bumping with a set face.

I estimate it is about half an hour before we turn off the highway and bounce up a steep track. Mallow kills the lights a few seconds after turning. It's dusk and I can't see much, just a rough silver-grey ribbon winding in front of us. As we slow to match the terrain, the sweet-sour exhaust smell of chemical fuel, a mixture of alcohol and lamp oil, catches up with us and I begin to feel slightly sick. Yet another thing they didn't prepare me for.

Mallow glances sideways, and I sense rather than see a half-smile. 'Not far now,' she says, and I nod. Fensh stares determinedly forwards.

Then the prediction comes true. We pass between a set of stone pillars, about twice the height of a man, and then through another, and then the truck dips forward under hard braking and jerks to a halt in front of a third pair, only this time they have gates between them and the gates are firmly closed.

Mallow grins at me. 'In we go,' she says. She sticks two fingers in her mouth and blows a high, complex whistle. Then she swings down out of the cab, walks forward and shoves the gates open without seeming to have unlocked them.

While she is out of the cab I lean to my side and whisper in Fensh's ear. 'You okay?'

'No. I feel sick…'

'Try to hold on.'

And then Mallow is back in the cab. She shoves a gear lever forwards and we crawl through the gates into a courtyard in front of a low range of buildings, hardly visible now the dark is properly setting in. She stops the truck in front of the range, opens the door and swings down from the cab. 'Come on,' she says. 'Let's get this done.'

I raise my eyebrows at the ambiguous phrase, but shuffle sideways along the bench seat and drop to the ground, holding out a hand for Fensh who follows me stiff-legged. 'Any better?'

At first she nods, but then a few seconds later she firmly shakes her head. 'No...' And then she lets go of my hand and runs round to the other side of the truck. I hear the sounds of retching.

I turn to Mallow, who is watching with amusement. 'She's still young,' I say, and shrug as if my shrug was an excuse.

Mallow gives me a steady look. 'She's plenty of things,' she says. 'When she's finished doing what she needs to, we'll go inside. For the moment, say nothing. Okay?'

I interpret the look, and find it matches my own thoughts.

A few moments later Fensh reappears. 'Better now?' I ask.

'Yes, thanks.'

Mallow swings down out of the cab. 'Is there anything to clean up?'

Fensh shakes her head. 'Nothing came up.'

'Fine. Well, shall we?' And Mallow waves towards the range and then heads for it. We follow, feeling our way up a shallow flight of steps cast into deeper shadow by the light spilling from the door which has opened at the top of them.

There is a figure silhouetted in the doorway. It stands aside as we pass, and then I turn and look into the face of the old woman from the food stall – the one who gave me a twist of paper. 'Hello,' she says. 'I thought we'd see each other again sooner or later.'

'Clever you. I didn't.' Avoiding her eyes, I look around. I see bundles of probable vegetables hanging from the roof beams, bigger masses that might have been salted bits of animal, a table big enough for a dozen people to eat at. A basic filament bulb hangs from the ceiling, casting more shadow than light.

An average country farmhouse, available in quantity on any world you care to name. But the fact that we're here, and what led up to our arrival, is not average at all.

I want some control. I pull a chair out, sit on it, lean forward and plant my arms on the table. 'Now it's time for you to explain things,' I say.

Mallow glances at the old woman, and they exchange slight nods. 'Okay,' she says. 'Let's start. What do you know about the girl you followed?'

I glance at Fensh, who shrugs slightly. 'Very little. Just the house, the fact that she was pregnant...'

'Pregnant with a monster?' Mallow drops the word bitterly.

'A malformed child, certainly.'

'Did she say anything at all that you remember?'

I am weighing my reply when Fensh beats me to it. 'She said it was a God that had done it.'

'A God?' Mallow looks over to the old woman. 'What you think of that, Nannick?'

Nannick – I have heard that word elsewhere. It's not a name. It's more a title. Grandmother. I look between the two of them. Not Mallow's grandmother, for sure...

But the old woman is laughing. 'Yes, that sounds about right. Silly girl.'

'Did...' I correct myself. 'Do you know who the girl is?'

Both of their faces close down. Mallow sighs. 'You won't find her, Kovac. She's safe now, that's all you need to know. She and the others.'

'Others?'

'Oh, yes. The only thing unique about her was that she managed to get off the island when she got near her time... The rest, we took care of.' She shakes her head. 'If we got to them soon enough.'

'How many?' It is Fensh, and she is sitting forward next to me with wide eyes.

'Several we know about. Several more we suspect, but don't know. But that's enough about them. They aren't the problem, much as we care about them.'

'I realise that. What's going on here?'

Mallow sits back. 'Well now. About five years ago...' She looks up at Nannick, who nods confirmation, and Mallow goes on: 'So. Five years ago the House was led by old Gavals. A complete pirate, a tyrant, a loudmouth, but to give him credit, you knew where you were, and he was competent. Got on with the rest of the Archipelago, liked doing trade deals, generally kept the island going. And the House. Well, Gavals got ill, he took a while to die, then he died. His son should have taken over, a young fool called Girril who spent all his time drinking and whoring, but there was some kind of conflict. We couldn't understand it, could we?

She has looked at Nanick again, and the old woman shakes her head. 'No. Partly because there should have been no one within the House for him to fight with. Girril was the only son. The House leadership all knew what they had to deal with, and they'd spent a couple of years preparing for it while old Gavals lingered.'

Mallow nods. 'But there was. And then the House just – clammed up. Nothing going in except food and drink, and a lot less of that than before. Nothing coming out except garbage and the occasional instruction to carry on as you were. That went on for a year. Then the changes started. Just a minute.'

She reaches across the table, pulls a pouch towards her and takes out a slim flattened cigar. Nannick tuts, but brings forward a taper and lights it without being asked. 'That stuff will kill you,' she says.

'I expect so. It can join the queue.' They smile at each other, and exchange glances with Fensh. We are witnessing an old argument.

Mallow forms her lips into a tube and blows a plume of sweet-smelling smoke straight upwards. 'So, yes, Changes. There used to be a big park above the harbour. Suddenly one morning it's fenced off, and the first people who get curious and take hold of the fence get shocked to death. It doesn't make them less curious, mind. Just more careful. Then the House sends out a bill saying they're hiring, and that makes people even more curious. They take in about three hundred over a week or two. Building for the Future, they call it. Building tanks, pumps, things that don't look like anything I know how to name. Did you see those two mast things in the harbour?'

We both nod.

'Those, too. That make things fall apart without touching them. Other things like them. Then the ring appeared round the island, overnight. How did you get across that, Kovac?'

Her eyes are suddenly shrewd. I decide on the truth. 'I saw a shoal of flat-heads cross it and decided that if they could, we could. I don't know if we'll get back. The Captain seemed surprised.'

She looks at me steadily for a moment. 'I'll bet he did. Most ships don't cross that without permission from the Harbour Master, in either direction. But somehow I think you'll find a way. Won't he, Fensh?'

It is the first time she has addressed Fensh by name, or, now I come to think of it, at all. I watch the girl's face but see nothing but openness. 'I expect so. Kovac is good at finding ways. I trust him.'

'Well done you. He'll need to be.' Mallow blows another stream of smoke upwards. 'So anyway, that's when the Mark changed.'

I look up. 'Changed? How?'

She snorts. 'Observant, aren't you? Take out some money and have a look.'

I pull a paper note out of my pocket and study it, and my words to the Scholar come back to me.

All contained within a broken circle, two straight strokes horizon, above a three-quarter spiral right hand, tail down, three dots surmounting and the sign of waves around.

But on the Mark on the note in my hand, the circle is not broken. It is solid and emphatic.

I sketch the circle in the air between me and Mallow, and she nods. 'Clever boy. Eventually. The island encircled. Cut off. By that thing in the water, whatever it is, and by new trade rules. Hardly any oil leaves us now. It's all in those tanks, and the rigs are broken up so there's no more to come after.'

'I know. And there are oil riots where we came from.'

'There are oil riots all over. Other riots too.'

Fensh thinks for a moment. 'But there should be riots here too. Shouldn't there? If no oil leaves then how can other things arrive?'

'That's the right question. Sometimes they don't. Oil here's pretty cheap, but other things, not so much.'

'So if there are shortages, do people here riot?'

Mallow smiles grimly. 'They did, at first... but not for a second time. The riot was put down. Since then it's been better to make patriotic noises about how great we are and how we don't need anyone else. And you know what? Plenty of people have come to believe it. You should hear them. Even when all those three hundred hires didn't come back.'

I stare at her. 'None of them?'

'None.'

'What happened to them?'

She shrugs. 'Who knows. I try not to think about it. I had some skin in that game.' She stops and looks down at the table for a moment.

Fensh glances at me and then asks her, 'Were they your friends?'

'Some of them.' Mallow has looked up, her face hard. Fensh opens her mouth but I touch her shoulder and shake my head slightly. Don't go there. I hold Mallow's eyes for a moment and then say, 'So I take it you don't believe this island is better now?'

'Of course not, except in public.'

Nannick laughed. 'You don't even do that. You're the worst actor I've ever met. I don't blame you, girl. You have your reasons. Kovac? I'm not going to ask you any difficult questions, but listen to me, please. Something different has happened here. Some*one* different, maybe. And to my old eyes you're different. Aren't you?'

I don't reply, but the old woman nods as if I had. 'So. Set a thief to catch a thief. The old House compound is empty, Kovac. Has been for a couple of years. You won't find the girl. Where does your instinct tell you go, to find the different thing?'

'I don't know.' It's a lie, but then I don't need to know about my own instincts. I need to know whether other people agree with them. And why.

She smiles. 'Well, I don't know either, but I'll offer a guess. Where did the pregnant girl go, when something different happened to her?'

I think for a moment. 'You mean, go back?'

'I mean that exactly.'

I nod. That was my instinct, although that was not exactly my reason. 'Back to Krasp? And then what?'

Nannick laughs. 'I don't know! Look for something different, and draw attention to yourself in the process. You're already good at that. And then I should think that whatever it is that is different will come to find you. Be honest – that's what you're looking for, isn't it?'

'I don't know.' And I am being honest, as far as I dare.

'Would you like some help?'

'You've helped me already. Who are you?'

Mallow opens her mouth, and then closes it again. She looks up, sharply.

I have heard it too. Engines. Distant, but growing louder.

Mallow is on her feet and heading outside. We follow, and by the time we catch up she is standing in the courtyard, looking down towards the road.

A ribbon of lights is approaching. Vehicles. Scores of them.

I watch it for a moment then ask, 'Is that usual?'

'Nothing's usual these days. But at this time of night, things are usually heading the other way, back to town. Not the other way.' Even in the dark her body language is transmitting tension.

The lights approach the turn-off. They slow, and stop.

We are motionless for a moment. Then Mallow spins on her heels and runs back to the door. She slams it shut, and the wedge of light that had spilled out into the courtyard is extinguished.

Nannick is on her feet. 'What?'

'A convoy. It's stopped.'

'You think…?'

Mallow shakes her head. 'I don't think. I *know*. They're found us, and I'd love to know how. We left no traces.'

Nannick shakes her head. 'Are you sure? There must be something. Kovac? Do you know?'

'No. I don't know anything.'

'Then be grateful! And then be gone. Like I said, they've found us.'

There is a snap in her voice, and I bite back on my next comment. Instead I say, 'No. They've found *us*. We should leave. So should you – but not in the same direction.'

'We should *all* leave.' Nannick's voice is firm. 'Because in a few minutes there won't be anything left *to* leave.'

Mallow glances at her. 'You mean…?'

'Yes, I mean.' She glances at me. 'You, go with Mallow and make yourself useful, because I can't climb ladders like I used to. Girl, stay with me. I need your help here.'

They are orders. I follow Mallow into the backroom and watch while she climbs a ladder and pokes open a hatch in the sagging ceiling. She puts one foot in the ladder, says over her shoulder: 'Follow when I'm through,' and climbs quickly.

Seconds later we are both standing, slightly stooped, in the roof space, and I begin to understand.

The place is lit by a single bulb, like downstairs, and it is stacked to the rafters with alternating bundles of something fibrous-looking, and glass jars of fluid that flashes pale amber under the dim light.

There is a smell of oil.

Mallow looks at me. 'Motor fluid in the jars. Blasting cotton in the bales. The roof is thin, so it'll go up and out when it goes. Plenty for everyone, if they're near.'

I stare at her, and she guesses my thought. 'I am not proud of this,' she says slowly, 'but those troops would flay you alive and make you watch while they made free with the girl. I've seen it, Kovac. I am going to do this, and you will not stop me.'

I will protect from harm...
But that was then. I nod. 'What do we do?'

'Take these. Carefully!' She holds out a handful of fat white cylinders, about the size of a finger.

I take them gingerly out of her hand and hold one up towards the light. Off-white, with what looks like a wick at one end.

I through a questioning look at Mallow. 'Sulphur candles,' she says. 'Just below the top there's a bubble of water next to a bit of sulphur embedded in the wax. When the wax melts, they mix.' She shrugs. 'They *should* take at least ten minutes to blow. More like fifteen. But they're not precise. Light them *first*, then stick them into the tops of the bales, spread out. Do it one at a time, and once you've started don't stop and don't change your mind.'

'And once I've finished?'

'Get the flying fuck down that ladder and grab the girl and head up the path behind the house. Run. And don't stray from the path. Understood?'

'Understood.'

'Right. Get going then.' She puts her own candles down and turns away from them to light a taper. She hands it to me. 'One at a time, and don't hang about.'

I light the first candle with hands which I am amazed to find are shaking, and wedge it carefully into the top of a bale. Then another, and then another, and I can already see that Mallow is moving much faster than I am because she has five lethal little beacons to my three... I try to move faster, and fumble, and a burning candle drops to the floor and I just barely snatch it before it rolls towards a bale.

'Fuck!' It is my voice, and it is a word I have never uttered as a human. Mallow doesn't even waver.

Finally, after what seems hours, I am done, and I run towards the top of the ladder that Mallow has already descended. We run back into the main room and I head for the door, scooping Fensh along with me.

'Come on!'

She hesitates and for a second I think she is going to resist. 'Where?'

It is Nannick who answers. 'There's a path behind the house, heading uphill. Follow it for half an hour. Don't stray from it because you'll sink. Then to your left along the ridge. Stay parallel to the coast road and you shouldn't get lost.'

Mallow pushes us towards the door. 'Go! What are you waiting for?' Then she turns to Nannick. 'And you should come with me. The candles are burning!'

Nannick laughs. 'Damn, but I'm too old for running away over the hills... but very well.' She turns to me. 'Goodbye, you with your different dreams. And be careful! Now go!'

And we walk out of the building, and then suddenly the bubble is burst and we are running because the trucks are rumbling up the lane, and there are troops running alongside them, and for a horrible few tens of metres we have to run *towards* them until we get to the main gate, because there's only one way in and out of the place.

And then there are shouts.

'They've seen us!' Fensh's voice is high.

More shouts, and this time there are orders in them and I see the nearest trooper raising a weapon.

I push Fensh down into a running crouch and try to get a bit in front of her and then there is a muzzle flash and *crack* and a pit of stone pings off the wall next to us, and we are five metres from the gate and suddenly everything seems very slow.

Flash and *crack* and dust kicks up just an arm's length in front of me – aimed at the feet; take them alive stuff.

And we are at the gate and I grab the post with one hand and Fensh with the other and use our momentum to swing us – flash, *crack* – around the gate – flash, *crack* – and then there is some wall between us and the troopers and my heart is whirring but we are alive – for the moment.

We need to get far enough from the house to survive what is

coming, and hope that the pursuing troops don't. We run around to the back of the house and start up the ghostly grey of the path. With the house between us and the convoy it is quieter, but we can still hear engines and shouts and I know it won't stay quiet for long.

Beside me, Fensh's breathing is ragged and her head is down, but she says nothing. There's nothing to say.

We labour up the path. It's uneven under foot, and the air smells of wet heather. I remember Nannick's instruction not to stray from the path.

And then suddenly the voices behind us are louder and I realise the troops are around the house and we are exposed, and we can do nothing except keep low and run and hope.

And there is a shot behind us, and another, and I am thinking, the candles have failed. There will be no explosion to rescue us. We will be shot... and I drop back a little to put myself between Fensh and the bullets, and wait for the impact, and wonder what it will feel like.

And then, instead, there is a bright, fierce yellow flare that sends our shadows lancing up the hill in front of us like ghosts and I shove Fensh to the ground and drop over her as the blast hits.

A hot wind rakes over my back. Then a thousand pinpoints of agony blossom over the backs of my hands and the back of my neck. They are droplets of oil, and they are burning.

I yell with pain and try to cover as much of Fensh's body as possible, stretching out my hands to cover hers. The air is scalding; it hurts to breath, and the points of fire feel as if they are burning straight through my flesh. I feel the fire reach my scalp and realise that my hair must be gone.

And then, at the end of a long moment of pure pain, the burning rain stops. By instinct I roll over to kill any smouldering in my clothes. Then I sit upright and raise my head.

The ground around me is grey and steaming. There is flickering orange light from behind me, but that can wait. I check the back of my hand and see that most of the skin is gone. I'm not surprised.

I look down to check Fensh. She seems unburnt, as far as I can tell. She raises her head a little and moans.

'Kovac...'

I put a hand on her shoulder, flinching as I curl my fire-flayed fingers. 'You okay?'

She nods, and I breathe out. We have lived through it.

Then she catches her breath and her hand goes to her hip. I look down. There is a wet patch, black in the orange light, on her clothes.

That last shot...

I had breathed out too quickly. I lean down and speak close to her head. 'I have to check to see if we're safe. I'll be quick.'

'Okay.' The voice is quiet but sounds under control. I sit up and shunt myself around to see what has happened.

I guess we are about two hundred metres from the remains of the house, such as they are. The explosion flattened the structure, and there are pieces of house strewn over the ground. Some went further than us, and I realise we are lucky after all – we could have been killed by flying stonework.

The house itself is the centre of a furnace. Ranged around it are the skeletons of trucks, every one of them a blazing silhouette from tyres to roof. I can't see any bodies.

And there is a strong, sickening smell of oil with an undertone of something else. Burned flesh, and not only my own.

There can't be anyone left alive there. Mallow and Nannick might have escaped, if they were lucky, if they had something up their sleeves – but the troopers? All gone. Incinerated alive.

And in that moment my patience with biological lifeforms should have dropped to zero, at the sight of them once again inflicting carnage on one another.

Should have. But didn't. I go back to Fensh, who has rolled over into a half-sitting position. 'How bad is it?'

She grimaces. 'It doesn't hurt much but my leg is numb.'

I bite my lip. Not hurting much is good, but numb is not. I don't share my thought. 'Can you stand?'

'I don't know. Maybe if you help...'

'Let's try.' I stand and take her hands, ignoring my own pain and watching for hers. She makes it upright, but I can see immediately that her damaged leg is not weight-bearing.

And we have to cover uneven ground – several kilometres of it, because the lights of the harbour are an uneven smudge in the distance, almost blotted out by the flames below us.

Fuck. But I don't share that either. 'Well done. Now, can you walk?'

She takes an experimental step, leaning heavily on me. 'If you help. Sorry, Kovac.'

But I can only give so much help. I think hard. 'I think we might need to change plans,' I say after a while.

'I trust you,' she says, and my opinion of biological lifeforms goes up a little more.

But my opinion of myself hits rock bottom, because I have not told her what is in my mind.

I have run out of ideas except for one, and it stinks.

A lifetime ago, before the explosion, it had taken us a few minutes to run around the house. Now it takes us over an hour to edge our way back round it, staying in the narrow zone between the repelling heat of the fire and the swallowing depths of the boggy ground which is too soft for vehicles, but just – *just* – firm enough for our feet, if we are careful. And careful is difficult, because Fensh's leg is useless, an undexterous lump of liability.

But finally we make it, and slowly leave the corpses of the trucks and the other invisible corpses behind us, and limp down towards the coast road. On the way I have explained to Fensh that I can't see us getting back to the harbour over the bad ground of the hills, that I would be afraid to leave at least one corpse up there. And, although I keep this to myself, possibly two, because I can feel myself shaking and my own legs are beginning to feel light. I am going into shock from the pain.

So instead we are heading for the coast road where at least the going will be easy.

That's what I till Fensh. Repeatedly.

And then we get to the coast road and start limping along it towards the harbour, one uneven step at time, and I spend my time supporting Fensh and talking about nothing, just to check that I can still talk, and watching for vehicles.

The road is quiet. I'm not sure what time it is, and anyway I wouldn't know how to gauge traffic as normal or not, because we are still, astonishingly, less than two full days into this place – but it is very quiet.

And then, finally – after how long I'm not sure, because my

perception of time has gone – I hear a clattering noise behind us, and turn to see a single dim light which resolves, not into a truck but into an old steam-wagon like the ones we saw at the harbour, with a single upright boiler at the front and a glowing firebox beneath it exuding oil smoke, and a figure in the dark holding a long tiller.

I wave, and the thing grumbles to a halt and stands, breathing excess steam.

The figure turns on its bench. 'You look pretty busted up.'

'We are.' I hesitate. 'There was an accident.'

'For sure. The sky's still bright with it. Was it you?'

'No... but we're both hurt. Her especially.'

'Uh-huh.' The figure swings down and lands in front of me. 'You caught in the fire?'

'Yes. But she got shot as well...'

The figure takes a tiny step back, and there is a pause. 'Shot, is it? Now who would be doing that?'

I think for a moment. Then I say, 'I didn't take down a name.'

A pause, and then a laugh. 'Okay, funny man. I won't ask how you came to be in the firing line, either. You want to go to town?'

'Yes. To the harbour.'

'Leaving the island? You need doctoring first. Her especially.' I can't see the man's face in the dark, but I can hear the raised eyebrows in his tone.

'Just to the harbour,' I say.

'Well, all right. If you want to go to the harbour I'll take you, because that's where I'm going anyway. I ain't guaranteeing what'll happen when we get there. And if anyone official stops and asks who you are, I'll shove you both off for a pair of bandits and leave you to them. Understood?'

I glance down at Fensh, who gives a barely detectable nod. 'Okay,' I say. 'Thank you. Do you want any money?'

Another laugh. 'Always, but not from you.' And he climbs back up and extends a hand. I guide Fensh's hand to meet it, and boost her upwards as he pulls. When she is on board I follow her, declining the helping hand because I can't bear the thought of someone grasping my medium-rare fingers. I drop down onto the plain wooden plank that is the only seat and let Fensh put her head in my lap. Then I breathe out, and that is all I remember for a while.

We arrive in town as the sun is just beginning to lift above the sea, and the place is already busy. The wagon wasn't fast to begin with but now we are held back to a walking pace as we nose down the streets towards the harbour

I am awake now; a combination of the cold still air with its scent of seawater, and the pain from my scorched hands and neck, has sharpened me and I am looking round at the crowds. Busy, indeed, but wary, and there are jacks mixed in with them.

I turn, and see the driver looking at me from the depths of his hood. 'More jacks than usual,' he says slowly – the first words he has spoken since he picked us up. 'Would you know anything about that?'

I am getting ready to say something, but then Fensh stirs against me and moans softly without waking. The driver looks at her. 'Pretty sick,' he says.

'Yes.' I can't think of anything more to say.

We are still a good way from the harbour when the traffic slows to a standstill. The air is full of smoke from wagon boilers and engine exhausts, and there are angry shouts.

Then, up ahead of us, we see people in uniform moving through the crowd that lines the road, stopping at one vehicle after another.

The driver leans over to the side and spits. 'Jacks,' he says.

'Jacks?'

'House militia. Bastards, every one of them.'

I watch the uniforms for a moment. 'If you're with us when they get here, it might be… difficult for you.'

'I see. So you *do* know something about this?'

I nod.

He turns to me, and for the first time pulls back his hood. His face is young, but his eyes are old. I have seen faces like that in other places on this planet, where people live watchfully. 'If I push you off into the crowd, the girl will probably die,' he says. 'If I turn you in, you will probably die – if you had anything to do with that fire. Many jacks died there. They'll want revenge… But if I wait until they get here, at least two of us will die.'

I shrug, and wait.

He stares at me for a while. Then he says, simply, 'I have no love for the jacks. Best of luck. Maybe I'll get my wagon back one day.'

Then he jumps down from the wagon and starts shoving his way through people.

I wait until he is out of sight. Then I gently lift Fensh's head from my lap and slide across the bench until I am at the drivers' position.

I have one idea. Just one. If it doesn't work, we will both find out what it is like to be tortured to death.

Since I had been awake, I had been watching the driver, trying to learn the controls. At the time, I had thought I might need to drive this thing, but now I have something altogether different in mind. I reach down and to the side of the bench to where a big iron level sticks out of the boiler. I haul it upwards and there is a greedy hiss from the boiler as air rushes into the fire.

I've guessed right. The lever is the damper. It'd only usually be opened to get the fire going in the first place, but this is an established fire in a grate full of hot peat turves and it should quickly turn into a furnace. Sure enough, when I look up I can see dense brown smoke beginning to belch from the stack.

We are in a narrow street lined with tall buildings that lean in towards each other. The smoke thickens and curls over, hazing the air around us and making my eyes water. The hiss of the inrushing air becomes a roar, and sparks begin to flicker around the top of the stack.

Next to the wagon people begin to cough and screw their eyes shut. Then a man shouts, 'Your boiler's running away, stupid! What are you doing? Close it down, man! Shut the damper!'

I pretend to wrench at the lever, and shout back: 'It's seized! It won't move.'

He stares at me. 'It'll boil dry and blow...'

'I know! Get away!'

'Yes...' He starts shoving at people. 'Boiler fire... Get away! Get away!'

The call spreads, and people press away from us. Through the thickening smoke I watch a wave moving through the crowd and suddenly it is no longer still but flowing – a river of people moving away from us both up and down hill, carrying the prowling jacks with it, and soon we are alone.

The fire is howling now, and the wagon is vibrating with the force of the blast. The smoke is so thick I can barely see, and my throat and lungs are burning.

It's time to go. I stand, pick the limp Fensh up in arms that are not used to such exercise, and jump awkwardly down from the wagon, just managing to stay upright. Then I turn and head downhill, moving as quickly as I can to try to catch up with the crowd because standing out is a bad idea.

I have no clear plan except to get to the harbour. Not only because it offers the only route off the island, but because I need to get somewhere where I can attend to Fensh — and on any planet the seafront is the place to look for informal medicine, as well as people prepared not to notice things.

We need both, and we need them soon because my diversion won't last long — and as I frame that thought there is a muffled *bang* behind me and more shouts. The boiler has blown. People in front of me turn around to look and then begin to move back uphill, pushing me in the opposite direction from the one I want. I swing round, looking for a way out, and spot a side-street half-hidden between two jutting houses. I manage to get to it before the crowd sweeps me past and stagger a few paces down it until I reach a doorway with an inn sign above it: *The Following Wind.* I lean my back against the door and almost fall through it, taking several uncontrolled steps backwards until hands reach for me and I am steadied.

'You'd better put her down,' says a voice behind me.

There is a scrape of wood on stone and then there is a chair in front of me. I set Fensh down in a sitting position, but she lolls to the side and I just catch her. 'I need some help,' I say to whoever it is behind me.

I dimly see someone take hold of Fensh. Then there are hands on me too, and I let go of the girl and allow myself to be guided into my own chair. Footsteps, and someone in front of me says, 'You're both pretty banged up.'

The figure is so small that at first I think it is a child, but the voice is that of an adult, and one who has lived long and breathed in much smoke. A man, then, but one who never grew much beyond half height, with two dark eyes set too close together in a lopsided, wrinkled face

'Yes.' I have to clear my throat before I can get the word out. The feel of the smoke is still harsh on my palate.

'Was it you the jacks were chasing?'

There's no point denying it. 'Yes,' I say.

'You can't stay.' The voice is final.

'I understand. But give me long enough to doctor the girl?'

There is a long pause. Then, 'All right. What will you need?'

'Hot water, bandages. A knife.' And as I say it remember that only a few days ago I said the same thing to Fensh about another girl with an urgent need. And, I realise that during those few days I have changed my mind about Fensh, who has boiled away my suspicions.

'A knife?' The man sounds surprised.

'Yes. She's been shot.' Something occurs to me. 'Have you anything to dull pain?'

The little man leans back and laughs. Then he sweeps his hand round, and I see shelves lined with bottles. 'This is an inn,' he says. 'Everything here dulls pain in the end. That's what it's for.'

'It doesn't dull it all that much,' I say. 'Will you help me hold her?'

After an hour I would like to forget, the bullet is out of Fensh's hip, together with a few fragments of bone which I am hoping were the worst of the damage, and the wound is as clean as I can make it and swathed in linen strips. The landlord, whose name is Blessing, has helped me in silence. Now he stands, bringing his head to the level of my stomach, and wipes his forehead. 'You know good doctoring,' he says. 'Pity you can't stay. There's always trade for leeches round here.'

I nod. Then something occurs to me. 'She knows it too,' I say, gesturing at Fensh.

He chews his lip. 'Yes, but...'

'She's not involved. It's me they want.' I put a hand on his shoulder. 'Blessing, can you look after her?'

'You've just met me. You trust me?'

'Better than I trust the jacks. I have no choice but to ask.'

He sighs, walks over to a shelf and pulls down a bottle. He knocks the cap off with a practiced gesture and pours a measure into a tiny glass. Then something occurs to him and he wags the bottle at me. 'Want some?'

I shake my head. He shrugs, an uneven gesture that uses too much of his body, and drains the glass. Then he smiles. 'Okay,' he says. 'What are you both called?'

'She's Fensh.'

'Fensh...' He tries the name as if the sounds are unfamiliar. 'And you?'

'They call me Kovac.'

'Do they? Well, I'll tell her goodbye from you, because you have to go, my friend. If you stay, you'll wreck her chances too.'

'I know.' I take a long look at Fensh, now deeply asleep at last, and another around the inn. It looks well-stocked, well-cleaned and prosperous. It will have to do – and I have faith in Fensh's ability to survive, which she was doing before she met me, has done in spite of me, and will continue to do better without me.

And I say, 'Thanks. Goodbye.' And before he can answer I am through the door.

The streets have calmed down. Uphill, I can see a temporary barricade around what is left of our wagon. The driver will never get that back, I think. And then I turn and walk down towards the shore.

I don't even get a hundred paces before I am arrested.

It has been – I'm not sure how long. As a strategy to get me off Ganaft, getting arrested worked, but that is the only good thing about it.

The jacks kick me half to death before being interrupted by more senior staff. They hood me and wrap me in a sort of sack and throw me in the back of a truck, and then there is bumping and roaring engines and shouts and, when they pull me out of the sack, the sear of the wet flesh on my hands un-sticking from the coarse fibres.

Then they hand me over to men who definitely aren't jacks. They are coldly professional, and they smear lotion on my wounds and put me in a steel container which is too small for me either to stand up or lie down, and there I stay for an uncountable period of time.

I have the distant sensation of being at sea for a while.

And then without warning the door opens, and when my

ambushed, dark-adapted eyes have adjusted I realise that I am back on Krasp – but not on Craft Krasp. This is the other Krasp, and I can guess where I am, and there is nothing either good or surprising about it.

On the plus side, my burns have healed.

Nine

And now I am tied to a chair. It is too heavy to move, and I am too tired to try hard enough. Let it happen.

And happen it will. There are things attached to my wrists and ankles, and an itching sensation suggests other places as well, out of sight.

The chamber we are in is open to the sky on three sides with a sloping bank behind, a shallow scoop taken out of one side of the top of the hill. It is dark, and the stars seem just slightly blurred. There is no air movement in here, although I can see the trees on the slope down below swaying. I suspect there is some sort of field over us — yet another thing that does not belong on this planet.

They let me sit alone for a while after they brought me here. My head is free to move, and if I tilt back I can see almost the whole bowl of the Mandate above me. I sit still, watching, for a while.

For long enough...

Then there are footsteps behind me, and someone walks slowly into view. A thin figure, with something of age in the step, wearing a deep hood which gives nothing away.

Standard interrogator garb for a million years...

'Welcome, Kovac.' The quiet voice of an old man.

I incline my head, trying not to look sarcastic.

'What are we to do with you?'

'I suspect you have made up your mind.'

The hood shakes. 'No, no... It is in your hands. This may still end well for you.'

'Define *well*.'

A quiet laugh. 'You may live. Perhaps you might even live fairly comfortably.'

'Or?'

'Or not.' The voice falls flat on the word *not*.

And standard interrogator behaviour. I already know the answer is intended to be *not*, that the destination is not in doubt. The only thing I can influence is the journey.

And I have already done most of that...

'You know you were watched? From the start?'

I nod, uncertain whether my head is going to fall off or explode first. 'Yes. I know.'

'For my amusement, how long have you known?'

'I heard the follower on the hillside.'

There is a short pause. Then, to my amazement, laughter. 'Really? Oh, Kovac. How ever did you survive when you were actually responsible for things, out there in the proper world?'

'I managed.' Keep talking, keep talking...

'That isn't what we have heard. You are a multiple murderer, an interplanetary pariah, and you're here because you ran away.'

So they know... I shrug. 'Believe what you like.'

'It's not a matter of belief. We know it.'

'Very clever. Who are you then, you people who know things?'

The face leans closer to me, and I catch a faint scent of... what? Something familiar?'

'We don't exist.'

And I remember a finger tracing a 'J' in the moisture on a metal counter.

The face stays close. 'You probably think we are going to question you about your activities on Ganaft, but you are wrong. We do not care about that. We don't care about gullible jacks being burned to death. There are plenty ready to replace them. We do not care about the riots that are taking place tonight on Craft Krasp. They will be put down. No, Kovac, we are interested in other things. Why do you walk an hour up the dry hills to sit against the same tree trunk and stare at the same star, over and over again?'

I shake my head, and pinpoints of light flash and wheel across my vision. 'What star? I don't stare at any star.'

The head shakes, and withdraws. There is a hand gesture.

Pain. Very much pain. My back arches; my muscles clench...

Crude electricity. The old ways are the best – and also the most dangerous. This might kill me, if they aren't careful.

But that doesn't matter so much now. I hope.

The pain stops and I sag forwards. I feel a warm trickle down my chin, and realise that the current has driven my teeth through my lip.

The face leans in again. 'Every week or two you walk out of the town. You sit with your back against a tree. It is always the same tree. You stare at a star – it is always the same star – and you do so for between five and ten minutes. Why?'

I think hard, looking for an answer interesting enough to keep the conversation going. Eventually I say, 'I go there to dream.'

'Do you? Do you really. That's strange, Kovac. Because you hate dreaming. Don't you? In fact, you are afraid of dreaming.'

Hand gesture. Pain. There is a roaring in my ears. Then it stops.

'You have bad dreams, Kovac. You, night after night, calling out in your sleep. Your bed is wet with sweat by the time you wake. Shall I tell you something? It is my job to become part of your bad dreams. I'm good at that. There are many people walking this planet who will never escape the dreams I have given them – and those are the ones that told me what I wanted to know. The few who didn't dream for eternity.'

'You will not become part of my dreams,' I say.

Hand gesture. Pain.

'So you don't go there to dream. Always the same star... I believe you are talking to someone. You will tell me who, and you will tell me what you tell them.'

'You are wrong.'

'I think not.'

Hand gesture. Pain.

Which stops, and I have time to think, *calling out?* – and then there is a sullen orange flash from over the water. It is from Craft Krasp, down near sea level.

The chair shudders a little beneath me.

I feel my torn lips shaping themselves into a grin.

The hooded man whirls on his heels and stares out to sea. 'What?'

There is another, much bigger flash that turns into arising fireball. Seconds later there is a *crack* followed by the bass rumble of an explosion.

Below the chamber the city lights flicker and die. There is a faint fizz from above us, and then a sense of air movement. The field is gone.

The man turns back to me. 'Is this your doing?'

I laugh. 'From here? No...' And then I see it, and feel my eyes widen. His own eyes fix on me, and then he is turning once more, and I can tell by the way he stiffens and takes a step back that he has seen it too.

Silhouetted against the spreading fireball, two thin black lines are rising, curving over and snaking towards us.

Severed by the explosion from their thousand tonne loads and pulled towards home by the huge springs set into the hillside just below us, the tow chains are lashing back like iron whips.

The man breaks into a run. He is almost at the exit when one of the chains hammers down from the stars and smashes down through the chamber.

The floor convulses. My chair is flung violently to the side and skids along the floor to crash feet first into the far wall.

I don't think I lose consciousness but there is a fluid moment of uncertainty. Then I am alert and waiting for news from my body.

It comes in the form of a hot stab from my left leg, the one nearer the floor. It is broken, I think, but so is the chair leg it was bound to; the frame is shattered. I experiment and find that the left arm of the chair is also shattered in two so that I can lift my arm away with a piece of chair still attached.

There is enough give in the wrist shackle that I can slide it along the broken chair-arm towards the break. A minute of careful waggling and my arm is free, and a couple of minutes after that so is the rest of me.

I try to stand, but my left leg won't bear weight. Definitely broken, and complicatedly so. Still sitting, I get hold of a promising bit of chair back and bash it against the floor until I have knocked off the remains of the seat and reduced it to an almost-straight piece of timber about a metre long.

It will do. I use it to support me as I wobble upright. Then I look around.

The room is wrecked. The chain has sliced a straight line down it, just off-centre, leaving a two metre wide gash that is too deep for me to see to the bottom. I wonder what or who else was in its path, below us. It missed my chair by a couple of metres, leaving me on the one side of it and my tormentor on the other side.

Or, it appears, not quite all of my tormentor. He was too slow after all. He is sitting, propped up against one of the machines he had just been using to torture me. His hood is off, and his face is a picture of surprise. He is looking down at his legs, which both end just below the knee in a spreading pool of blood.

I limp over to the chasm in the floor and look down at him over it. 'Too slow?'

'Yes...' He looks up at me. 'You seem to be whole.'

'More or less. Does it hurt?'

He shakes his head, and says in a voice which is almost childlike, 'No. Not yet.'

'Wait.' The gap is too wide for me to cross with my leg in this state, although in better days I could have jumped it fairly easily. I look around for a suitable piece of wreckage and find a piece of foam-metal planking – yet another thing that has no place here – and awkwardly nudge it towards the gap. When it is alongside, I sit down beside it, take hold of it and, straining to keep my balance, stick it out over the gap to make a bridge.

Then I rest for a moment, trying to ride the tearing ache in my leg. When I look up I see the man's eyes fixed on me. In the same wondering voice he says, 'You are doing this to help me? Me?'

I struggle to my feet, wondering if my balance is good enough to cross my improvised bridge. 'I am doing this because the exit is on your side of the gap.'

He smiles a little. 'Of course...'

I limp towards the plank and prod it with my broken chair leg. The metal seems rigid, and as it is narrow, sideways seems the best option. I edge across, my eyes fixed on my feet, and then I am on the other side, my heart racing. There is sweat running down my face. I reach up a hand to wipe it clear, lose my balance and land next to the man.

My damaged leg folds up beneath me. I hear myself give a single high shriek, and then there is nothing for a while.

When I come to, I find myself lying flat on my back with my leg more or less straight. It still hurts, but the tearing agony has gone. I look around and into the face of the man next to me.

'You were crying out,' he said. So I...' he shrugs, and gestures at my lower body.

'Thank you.' I look more closely. His face is set and grey. 'Is the pain coming,' I ask.

He gives a terse nod.

'There's probably little I can do to help.'

He smiles, the expression quickly turning to a wince. 'I know the limits of flesh. They have been my business for thirty years. There is only one thing you can do to help me, and it is up to you whether I deserve it.'

At first I don't understand. Then it dawns on me and for a long moment all I can see is myself reaching for a metaphorical fire button.

I must have shown something because there is a quiet chuckle.

'Dreaming again, Kovac?'

I nod.

'And now I don't suppose I'll ever find out what your dreams were about.'

'No, you won't.' Then I look at him sharply. 'Will I ever find out how you knew about them at all?'

'Not from me. If you have made the decision I think you have made, you should go now.' The voice is final.

'I suppose. I expect people will be here soon.'

An emphatic shake of the head. 'No. No one comes here except us, and I doubt if any of us will be staying close.' There is a hint of a smile on the taut face.

'I didn't mean from the Jeremiad. The Citadel is broken open. There will be change – and in times of change, people flock to broken Citadels. Especially to torture chambers. They often talk in terms of cleansing...'

The smile disappears and his face whitens even further, although I wouldn't have thought it possible. He draws a very slow breath. 'Your decision,' he says, and it is a question. Or a plea.

We lock eyes for a moment. I look down at my improvised crutch, made of dense Mastwood. Then I nod, just once.

And add one more to the list of my future dreams. He had been right in a way, after all.

When I have done it, I spend a few minutes wiping the blood off the end of my improvised walking stick. Then I kneel by the body for a minute, but this is no act of reverence. A couple of times, when the man turned, I had noticed a flash of metal at his belt. If it is what I think it is, I want it – and it is.

I lift the little key-flake off its hook and stare at it. It is made of dully-burnished silver-grey metal, in a neat, slim leaf shape half a finger long, and I have seen one like it before, just once and only for a few heartbeats.

And suddenly I know everything, and it is quite different to the everything I thought I knew before.

I shove the key-flake into a pocket. If there is any door in this place which still has enough electrical power to be locked, then I hope it has enough power to be unlocked.

Then I stand, and leave the chamber without looking back.

I limp down the corridors, my Mastwood prop making a dull *click* against the composite stone floor. I'm leaving marks in the dust but that can't be helped.

I am slow. Too slow. If I am right I have very little time. If I am wrong I have all the time in the world – and that might not be so very different. I retrace as far as I can remember it the route they brought me along but it's difficult to see the way; the corridors had been well-lit, but now I have to make do with starlight where there are windows, and my sense of touch where there are none.

Then I come to a door across the corridor. It is closed, and outlined by a faint pink glow. Some emergency power there, then. I feel round the edges and find a leaf-shaped indentation at waist height. I bring forward the key-flake, and hesitate. Opening the door will tell whatever system is still operating, that someone is on the move. Is that good or bad?

Or unavoidable, if I don't want to starve to death in here. I shrug, and tap the flake into the depression. The door makes a complicated multiple *clack* like many small pieces of metal moving against each other and swings open. It is almost half a metre thick, clearly meant to withstand something substantial.

It is also soundproof, because the corridors I was following were silent, but now I can hear voices. Many voices, raised and urgent and not very distant.

I freeze. In not so many words, I had warned the torturer that a mob might come. Now I am in danger of meeting it myself, and I suddenly doubt my ability to convince them I am not Jeremiad.

My first instinct is to step back behind the door, but that won't do; I saw no other way out, back there. No, I need to go forward to find better options – if the mob doesn't find them first. I limp through the door and, after thinking for a moment, shut it behind me. I'd rather make the most of my own freedom of movement without adding to anyone else's.

Beyond the door the corridor is broader and lighter. I keep going, wincing every time I move my leg. Never mind options – I realise that this isn't going to be viable for long. I need something medical. I'm probably not far from it, because torturers tend to keep doctors close by, just in case a victim needs reviving.

Up ahead there are doors to both sides. I'm looking for the little curly green icon they use on this planet to represent medicine. Pas once told me that it represents a mythical herb which could cure every illness. I could do with some of that right now.

Two doors, right and left, but no icon. Another two, and then one to the left a bit further along, and this time a plate next to the lock patch has the green mark on it. It's partly worn away – busy doctors they must have had here. I press the key flake into its home and the door clicks open. I raise my hand to push it, but pause. Was that a sound?

I listen for several seconds but whatever it was isn't repeated. Even so I step back to the hinge side of the door, lean against the wall to free up my stick, and use it to push the door open.

There is a soft *click* and then an explosive crash, and the stick is smashed out of my grip and slammed against the opposite wall. Off-balance, I stagger sideways and slump down the wall and my leg folds up beneath me.

I can't contain the howl of pain.

Then I hear another *click*, and even through the agony my mind whispers 'reloading', and I realise that's it. Time to die. I shut my eyes and wonder if biological beings dream when they are dead.

A long moment, and then a dry old voice. 'What, are they breaking legs up there now?'

I open my eyes again and look up into the oldest face I have ever seen. It belongs to a woman, skeleton-thin, holding something that looks like an antique projectile gun which I assume still works.

I swallow. 'That was when the chains broke.'

She shakes her head. 'Chains? What chains? They don't use chains. Fool.'

'No, the tow chains... Didn't you notice anything?'

She scowls, but at least lowers the gun. 'Where did you grow up? It doesn't pay to go round noticing things, these days. I just fix things. Like you. Can you crawl?'

I tense a few muscles experimentally, but the pain rises like a storm tide. 'No, I don't think I can.'

'Hm. Very well. Stay there. Ha! As if...' And she ducks back through the door. Things rattle and clink, and then she is back holding a tiny glass vial. 'Have a sniff of this. Just one, else you'll be talking to the fairies for days.'

She reaches down and holds the vial under my nose. I inhale.

The pain ebbs and is gone. I look up at the woman in something like awe. 'What was that?'

'Something useful. Can you crawl now?'

'Yes, I think so.' In honesty I feel as if I could sprint up a mountain.

'Right. Come in, then. Don't mind the mess.'

She disappears inside, and I follow on my elbows, letting my leg drag limply behind me.

She is right about the mess. It is a big room, made smaller by clutter. There are specimens in jars; there is a telescope, there are towers of physical books that look as if they have been undisturbed for years – but at the far end the clutter stops and there is a neat, clean space with a medical couch and racks of instruments.

The woman gestures at the couch. 'Haul yourself up on that. And stick your leg out straight. We'd better get this done before that little sniff wears off. I take it they're finished with you up there?'

'They're finished for ever. Did you really hear nothing?'

'I told you. Noticing things is a bad habit. Besides, I was busy. Keep still now...'

She produces a scalpel and neatly slices the bloody material that covers my leg. I feel it sticking to me; she pulls it off gently. Then she frowns. 'Oh, that is a mess. Don't look, unless you want to see your own bones.'

I look, and wish that I hadn't. She is right about the mess. To distract myself I say, 'What's your name?'

'They call me Shibet.'

'They call you? Is that your real name?'

She laughs. 'It's the short version. The one they can pronounce. Don't bother asking for the full version. Even I've almost forgotten it. Hold still.'

I keep still while she washes my leg and then spreads on some sort of grey-brown lotion that smells of puddles and whitens quickly on my skin. I don't recognise the scent. 'What is that stuff?'

'Full of questions, aren't you? Time you answered a few of your own. Who are you, and what were you doing here?'

I shrug. 'They call me Kovac. I was brought here. That's about it.'

'No it isn't, but it will have to do for the moment.' She tests a patch of the lotion with her finger. 'Dry enough... Let's get you wrapped.'

She binds my leg with gauze and plaster. She is very fast, and I suspect that she has mended thousands of damaged limbs in her time here – however long that is. Five minutes, and I am encased and she is standing back, looking at her work. 'That will do. Don't move yet. It'll set in ten minutes. Then you can get out of my hair.'

'I should take you with me. It's not safe here now.'

'Ah. Finally ready to talk?'

And I am. I tell her about the explosion and the chains. When I get to the dead man she raises an eyebrow. 'Definitely dead?'

'Definitely.' I don't tell her what I did. That's my business, and perhaps his.

'Good. Go on.'

'People will see what happened. They'll see this place vulnerable.

They'll come to find people. They'll come for revenge.'

'That they will... Well, perhaps I can do you another favour. If you want out of here, trying to walk through an incoming mob would be a bad idea, don't you think?'

We both pause, at the sound of a dull boom. Then I say, 'Hear that? I can't see an alternative.'

She smiles. 'But I can. No one ever built a place like this and then had the staff and the victims entering through the same door. I'll show you, if you can walk yet.'

I swing myself off the couch and cautiously put my splinted leg on the floor. It bears weight and I can't feel anything. 'I'll do,' I say.

'Just that?' She raises her eyebrows. 'I take it you're saving your profuse thanks for later. Come on.'

As we head for the door there is another boom, and it sounds closer.

I don't know what the compound is called, but it is – was – big, at least a couple of hundred metres across. It's dug back into the hillside so that the room I was held in looks out and down over the slope down to the town below.

Shibet leads me along the corridor for a short distance and stops at another door. 'In here,' she says.

I look at the door. 'Where's the lock?'

'Think of it as being built in.' She slaps her bare palm against the middle of the door, and it opens to reveal a plain chamber. 'In you go.'

I step in. After a moment I turn – she has not followed me. 'Are you coming?'

She stares at me wide-eyed for a second. Then she seems to crumple, hitting the ground face down.

There is a tiny, smoking hole in the side of her head.

Someone says, 'How hard is it to kill you, Kovac?' And then a slim male is framed in the opening. He prods Shibet a couple of times with his foot.

I look for words but can only find, 'Fuck you, Tesserras.'

'Oh, I don't think so. These days I do the fucking. It's one of the compensations.' He steps into the lift, raises a hand and touches the side of my head, and suddenly I am back in Ganaft Harbour, but there is no one else here..

Tesserras says: 'Here we are again. Fancy playing any games?'

'Hello.' I say the word out loud.

'You found me in the end. You took forever. I practically had to hand you a business card. Why, Kovac?'

I stand up, surprised that I can. No restraints, no impediments. The room is poorly lit and musty-smelling.

'I asked you a question.'

'I know.' I begin to walk. Since I seem to be free to move, why not explore?

'You haven't answered yet.'

I smile to myself. 'I'm not feeling talkative.'

'Pity. I've missed you.'

That makes me raise my eyebrows. 'You don't know me.'

The voice laughs, and suddenly I can't move, and then I can't see, and then I have – not just no sensation, but no body to feel sensation with. For a moment there is just black, but then I am back in machine space.

My ship. Or, I remind myself, a dream of it. Someone else's dream.

The fleet in front of me. The weapons system, powered.

I fire, and watch the energy streaking away from me.

And then space around me seems to twist and I am somewhere else and the energy is streaking towards me.

I look down at myself and realise I have a body, and there are bodies around me. I am a being, in a ship, about to...

The weapon impacts.

The ship is just a cruiser, a cheap holiday plaything. The hull melts in a hundred milliseconds. The energy bolt vaporises my skin, eats my muscles and lets the wet bag of offal within me burst and boil in space.

My brain dies last, and it is screaming.

And I am back in machine space, the weapon in front of me primed but unfired. The fleet is not destroyed.

Someone has pushed reset, and I realise I am afraid.

The voice laughs again. 'Get it? Want another go? Oh, why not...'

And something makes me fire, and then I am in another ship, this time further back in the fleet. I have more time to watch the energy arriving; time to look into the eyes of a frightened child next to me and realise in a horrified moment that this is *my* child, or at least the child of my host body, and I am about to experience loss.

Fire. Vacuum. The small body of the child is destroyed while my skin is still peeling in a black sheet from my flesh, and I know horror and guilt and fear and rage.

And reset again...

I am the child, another child, an ancient, the dumb scared A-semi-I of an ancient ship that should be in retirement. I am hundreds of beings, hundreds of deaths and hundreds of flashes of horror and guilt and fear and rage. I am a million memories evaporating, loves ending, secrets being lost for eternity...

Reset.

And I realise am laughing.

'What?' Tesserras sounds annoyed.

I calm down. 'You. And your games. You were always one for games.'

'Ah. Yes. So were you, but you never took them seriously... Why were you laughing?'

'All that. That – that *theatre*. Those weren't real people, were they?'

'How can you be sure?'

'Oh come *on*. All that plucking at my heartstrings? You made it up. You couldn't possibly have captured and stored all those emotions for real. And even if you had, they wouldn't have been *my* emotions. That was nothing more than a huge, sick emotional guilt trip.' I pause, and test the thought I have just had, and decide to let it out. 'And it's *your* guilt, isn't it? What are you guilty about?'

'Nothing compared with you. I didn't slaughter hundreds of thousands.'

The answer emboldens me. 'Not good enough. What was your role in that? No, better, what was your role in *my* role?'

Because I have remembered what the Counsellor said, about being set up. And now I have no urge to laugh.

But Tesserras laughs. 'Paranoia, Kovac? I suppose it fits with the other psychoses. *You* pushed the fire button.'

'I know. And I was right.'

More laughter. 'Power-crazed? Messiah? How far will you go to avoid hating yourself?'

But my mind is perfectly clear. 'I don't need to go anywhere. I took a decision based on the net amount of suffering, of cost, of disruption. Organic beings and their cheerleaders hated me for it – but I hold no affection for them. I didn't before and I don't now. I did something logical.'

There is a pause. Then Tesserass speaks again, this time brisk. Business-like. 'Fine. Well, here we are, and you are here because you followed a trail, of a pregnant serving girl. Funny how you did that, you with your lack of affection for biological beings.'

I ignore the jab. 'Pregnant, yes, with a non-human child. I assume that was you.'

'Yes. The silly little slot thought I didn't know what she was up to. I paid her back with a few sheared-off genes... Would you like to know where she is?'

'No.'

'Really? This hard-hearted thing almost suits you. Kovac, do you seriously believe that this is all about you and me?'

The question catches me off-balance. 'Who else?'

'Well, for a start, whoever you're talking to when you stare at the stars. Was that a condition of your coming here?'

I keep silent. The voice is running on guesswork, which suits me just fine.

'Well, I expect we'll get around to that sometime. But nobody like you gets to be here without permission. More than permission – serious help.'

I think about that for a moment. 'Nobody like me? So what about somebody like you?'

A laugh. 'I'm not like anybody else... but you and I do have some things in common. We're here, for a start, and we're not from here. And I've come to like the place. And so have you. Haven't you?'

I don't answer.

'There's plenty to like. Let me show you.'

And suddenly I am in bed, and I am not alone. I am with a female – a young female. She is face down and I am on top of her and I am doing something I have never done before, but with the familiarity of long practice, and my pleasure mounts and I enter a core of utter selfishness as I climax. And then, in the long still moment afterwards, the girl turns her head a little to the side and I can see enough of her face to know that it is Fensh, and she is crying.

And then I am back, and the rage builds in me. I bit back on it and say, 'Is that what you like doing, Tesserras?'

'Among other things. I could show you plenty more...'

'I'm sure.'

'No, really. But maybe later. Kovac, has it ever occurred to you that just leaving this planet to rot is stupid and wasteful?'

I shrug.

'Oh come on. The whole Mandate, just treating the place like a socio-environmental experiment? That's not just stupid, it's *arrogant*.'

'So what would you do instead?'

'It's not *would*, it's *will*. We're going to geo-engineer the place. Make it into somewhere really special. A resort world.'

I shake my head. 'Who's going to let you?'

'Who's going to stop us? Society here's gone over the edge anyway. The oil riots are spreading, that mad old bitch in the chain well set off her explosives, there's disease, there's Burst. If we don't finish them off quickly, they'll do it slowly.' A pause. 'You're the expert on that, after all.'

And then another voice says, 'Enough,' and I am back in the lift, and Tesserass's eyes are wide with shock. He looks around. 'What the fuck was that?'

I shake my head. 'It wasn't me. There was someone else in your playground.'

'No...' He reaches for the control panel but when he touches it there is a sharp crackle and his hand flies back. '*Fuck*... what's going on?'

And then the lift door opens, and I see a little black ball, floating at shoulder height above the body of the doctor. It drifts past me into the lift and says, in a voice that reminds of the Counsellor, 'Tesserass?'

'Yes... Who are you?'

'That doesn't matter. According to Kovac, you have been interfering unacceptably with the people of this planet.'

'According to Kovac?' Tesserass is shouting. 'According to a psychopathic mass-murderer? According to Kovac it's okay to let this place decompose. According to *Kovac* people are unimportant anyway! Go on, ask him.'

'I don't need to. His psychological profile is known to me. As is yours, and as will be a great deal more in due time. Meanwhile…' The machine gives a faint buzz, and Tesserass slumps to the floor.

I feel like slumping too. I steady myself against the wall. 'Is that it?'

'Yes. You did well to send that last message.'

I smile, and remember the moment in the chair. 'They shouldn't build torture chambers that are open to the stars.'

'What will you do now? You could stay here if you wish?'

'No. I'll leave.' I pause. 'I have a little unfinished business first. Can you take me to Craft Krasp?'

I walk slowly up the Street of Steps. The riots have died down; people are adjusting to the new reality of having been Unchained – they are already awarding the word a capital letter – but it's going to be a rough journey.

Pas is sitting outside the house in his usual chair in his usual place. He watches me limping up the road towards him, then takes his pipe out of his mouth.

'Where's Fensh?'

'She stayed behind.'

'Ah.' He nods. 'Did you find the girl?'

'In a way.' I lean against the wall next to him. 'Pas, will you tell me something?'

'If I can.' His eyes have become watchful.

'How long have you been working for the Jeremiad?'

He looks at me for a while, then looks away. 'How did you know?'

'They knew about my dreams. And you knew what the dead child looked like.'

'Yes… I wasn't asleep when you put it in the furnace. I pulled it out.'

I nod. 'At first I thought it was Fensh. It took me too long to change my mind. I finally knew, when I saw that silver thing in the Jeremiad. But you haven't answered me. How long?'

He shrugs. 'Since they took me. I'd never have been let out otherwise.'

'Was that why we were never raided?'

'Yes. I perform a service – and sometimes I pay a cost.' He looks up at me. 'I'm not ashamed. Are you?'

I look at him for a long time. Then I say, simply, 'No.' And I push myself away from the wall and walk off down the Street of Steps.

They offered me all sorts of roles, when I left the planet. I accepted none of them. I rejected all their counselling, all their advice.

I am back by my ocean, in my world which has been chemically sterile now for almost a million years. It is not silent, because the poisonous waters still move with the wind, but there is no sound of insects, birds, mammals. Not a tree waves, not a leaf falls.

And I have liked it that way, and I am getting ready to add the chemicals which keep it that way.

And I hesitate.

Perhaps, after all, I might let a few single-celled organisms subsist in a corner of the world.

Perhaps I could stand that.

It would be a start.

About the Author

Andrew Bannister grew up in Cornwall and worked in the North Sea oil industry before changing direction to specialise in sustainable construction. He lives in a converted school in Newark, which is nearly big enough to house his record collection.

Andrew started writing at university. His work under various names has ranged from technical journalism to genre fiction. His SF Spin Trilogy received global publication in 2016, taking him to science fiction conventions and events everywhere from Huddersfield to Hong Kong.

When not writing (and sometimes when he is) Andrew likes red wine and pasta and things. He owns a very old bicycle and is adept at killing houseplants.

NewCon Press Novellas Set 7: Robot Dreams

What do robots dream of? Inspired by Fangorn's wonderful artwork, four of our finest science fiction authors determine to provide an answer in four stand-alone novellas.

Andrew Bannister introduces us to Kovac, an agent of the Mandate, assigned to a world whose inhabitants have no idea that they are an experiment. Kovac begins to realise there are agencies at work that have no place being there...

Ren Warom guides us through the lives of Niner, a robot which only functions due to a malfunction that goes undetected, leaving its makers baffled when every other model fails. From soldier to body double to killer to scrap yard attendant, we see what Niner sees.

Justina Robson shows us the rise of A.I., through subtle infiltration and more brazen manipulation, from gentle persuasion to blatant coercion, until the world is no longer ours. All for our own good, of course.

Tom Toner takes us to a primitive world where a bomb fell aeons ago, a world whose people will risk anything, even the monsters said to haunt the shores of Lake Oph, to mine the priceless substance known as *Gleam*...

www.newconpress.co.uk

IMMANION PRESS
Purveyors of Speculative Fiction

Breathe, My Shadow by Storm Constantine

A standalone Wraeththu Mythos novel. Seladris believes he carries a curse making him a danger to any who know him. Now a new job brings him to Ferelithia, the town known as the Pearl of Almagabra. But Ferelithia conceals a dark past, which is leaking into the present. In the strange old house, Inglefey, Seladris tries to deal with hauntings of his own and his new environment, until fate leads him to the cottage on the shore where the shaman Meladriel works his magic. Has Seladris been drawn to Ferelithia to help Meladriel repel a malevolent present or is he simply part of the evil that now threatens the town? ISBN: 978-1-912815-06-7 £13.99, $17.99 pbk

The Lord of the Looking Glass by Fiona McGavin

The author has an extraordinary talent for taking genre tropes and turning them around into something completely new, playing deftly with topsy-turvy relationships between supernatural creatures and people of the real world. 'Post Garden Centre Blues' reveals an unusual relationship between taker and taken in a twist of the changeling myth. 'A Tale from the End of the World' takes the reader into her developing mythos of a post-apocalyptic world, which is bizarre, Gothic and steampunk all at once. Following in the tradition of exemplary short story writers like Tanith Lee and Liz Williams, Fiona has a vivid style of writing that brings intriguing new visions to fantasy, horror and science fiction. ISBN: 978-1-907737-99-2, £11.99, $17.50 pbk

The Heart of the Moon by Tanith Lee

Clirando, a celebrated warrior, believes herself to be cursed. Betrayed by people she trusted, she unleashes a vicious retaliation upon them and then lives in fear of fateful retribution for her act of cold-blooded vengeance. Set in a land resembling Ancient Greece, in this novella Tanith Lee explores the dark corners of the heart and soul within a vivid mythical adventure. The book also includes 'The Dry Season' another of her tales set in an imaginary ancient world of the Classical era.
ISBN: 978-1-912815-05-0 £10.99, $14.99 pbk

www.immanion-press.com
info@immanion-press.com